EVERYTHING IN THIS HOUSE
BREAKS

ABOUT THE AUTHOR

Sandra Bunting grew up on the east coast of Canada and was awarded a BA in Radio and Television Arts from Ryerson in Toronto. After working for CBC News, Toronto, she moved to Europe and lived in France, Spain, and Ireland. She received Masters in Writing from National University of Ireland, Galway. Her first poetry collection, *Identified In Trees*, was published there by Marram Press. Her first collection of short stories, *The Effect Of Frost On Southern Vines* was published in 2016 by Gaelóg Press. This is her second collection.

Sandra is currently on the editorial board of the Galway based literary magazine, *Crannóg* and at the helm of her own independent publishing imprint, Gaelóg Press. She is a member of the New Brunswick Writers' Federation and the Galway Writers' Workshop.

In 2012 she was awarded a Glenna Luschei award for poetry through the 'Prairie Schooner', University of Nebraska. She was runner-up for the 2006 Welsh Cinnamon Press First Novel Competition and was a finalist at the 2009 Irish Digital Media Awards for her Blog: *Writing a Novel Online*.

www.sandbunting.com

ALSO BY THE AUTHOR:

Identified in Trees (Poetry)
The Effect of Frost on Southern Vines (stories)

The Claddagh – Stories from the Water's Edge (co-author with
Edith Pieperhoff, Evelyn Diskyn and Paul Malone)

EVERYTHING IN THIS HOUSE BREAKS

stories

Sandra Bunting

Everything In This House Breaks
Published by Gaelóg Press
409 Burnt Church Road
Burnt Church E9G 4C9
New Brunswick, Canada
gaelogpress@gmail.com

www.SandBunting.com
sandra.bunting@gmail.com

ISBN 978-0-9880992-1-0

The characters and events portrayed in this book are
fictitious. Any similarity to real persons, living or dead, is
coincidental and not intended by the author.

Thanks to the editors of Crannóg, Criterion, Blinkzine,
Carillion, dANDelion and Siar Press in which some of
these stories were first printed.

Book and Cover Design: www.Cyberscribe.ie

TABLE OF CONTENTS

TABLE OF CONTENTS (CONTD)

EVERYTHING IN THIS HOUSE BREAKS

September crept in with its warm wand and painted everything a burnt gold and fiery orange. I had started a job doing household surveys for an economic research company. It gave me a little extra money and I could make my own hours. My area was a pleasant residential estate near the centre, where I called on each house with my black leather bag and my laptop asking questions about heating, electrical appliances and plumbing. Sometimes I would bring my little dog with me.

I soon found out that it wasn't as easy as I thought it would be. If people weren't there, I had to call back. I never knew if the house was unoccupied, if the residents were away, or if they were just out a lot and I had to find the right time to catch them. Neighbours weren't much help. Although there was a definite sense of community, there were no busybodies. No one could tell me much about the people next door.

"Why don't you talk to Joe Mc Enree in Number 10?" someone suggested.

"He's been on the residents' committee for years," someone else said.

"Go to Joe. He knows everything," another said.

I walked up to number ten. It was a house much like the others but it had been freshly painted, the trees and hedge in the yard were immaculately trimmed, the window boxes and hanging baskets still in flower. Tall cacti basked lazily in the sun porch. I rang the bell. I rang it again. Some people I had to deal with were a bit deaf, and according to the neighbours, Joe McEnree was not young.

The inside door opened forcefully. A man walked on through the sun porch to open the outside door. He was a big man. You could imagine him as a lumberjack or a miner in the wilds of Alaska although he was a bit stooped now. He brushed his white hair from his forehead.

"My wife is sick," he said accusingly. He meant to whisper but it was hard to contain his strong voice. He was a man used to speaking loudly.

I explained what I was doing. Eventually, flattered by what the others on the street had said of him, he stepped aside to let me in.

"If you are quiet you can come into the kitchen," he said. "My wife's sleeping now."

The kitchen was spotless. He made a pot of tea while I got out my visiting list.

We went through it and he told me what houses were vacant and what the best time was to catch the more elusive ones.

"It's not that I spend all my days peeping out the window. They come to me for things."

"That's an honour," I said.

"It has taken a long time," he sighed. "When I came here first I'd put out a hanging basket. The kids would knock it down and destroy it. I'd put another one up, the same thing. Finally after about six or so, they got tired and left it alone."

He got up and turned the radio on.

"The All-Ireland. Must catch a bit of that. The same thing with the common green," he went on. "I'd plant trees, they'd destroy them, and I would plant them again. I have a stubborn nature I guess. Now everyone is putting window boxes out themselves. We might go in for the most improved neighbourhood competition next summer."

I thanked him and told him I'd see him in the spring. He had filled me in on all the neighbours and I was able to find them in by going at the times he suggested. I knew the houses that were vacant and didn't bother returning there. Joe McEnree had saved me from wasting a lot of time.

****

It was a bad winter. There was hardly a dry day. Wind struggled violently with the windows, puddles grew larger and darkness seemed to be eternal. Spring was not much better but daylight was struggling for the upper hand. It was time again for the survey. I had to interview the same people I had before and note any changes: the addition or demise of pets, changes in the type of heating system, a second car or television. I went to Joe McEnree's house first. He answered the door immediately. I found him looking older and slightly more stooped.

He asked me in and, on passing the sun porch on the way to the kitchen, I remarked how magnificent the cacti were. They seemed to be taking over the room.

"I've never really taken to them," he said. "It was my wife that liked them. Now that she's gone, I keep them because she liked them."

"I'm so sorry about your wife," I said. "I didn't know."

"It's for the best. She was in pain. But I'm fierce lonely without her. Ah well. We have to go on."

We went through the questions on the survey and duly noted the changes. One occupant, not two at number 10. He told me other changes to the area and then he perked up.

"We have entered the improved neighbourhood competition," he said. "You must look at the new garden I planted at the side."

I recognized the lilies, hydrangeas and poppies, but there were many others I didn't know. I could imagine the mix of colours when all the plants were blooming. I would certainly give him the prize for this garden. If everyone in the neighbourhood did something similar, it would be spectacular.

"Number nineteen is starting an old-fashioned herb garden surrounded by lavender bushes. Another house is specializing in roses." He was beaming.

I had to go back briefly in summer to clarify one of the questions. The little estate looked beautiful. The scent of lavender mixed with rose, lily and lilac wafted around the corner before the full colours of the blossoms hit.

"We won," Mr. McEnree said. He saw the blank expression on my face and impatiently reminded me.

"The Improved Neighbourhood Competition. We won. I have a thousand euro cheque." He couldn't contain his smile.

"I'm going to spend it on a little bench and maybe a border around the green."

It was September again before I got back to the area. There was a new survey. I was surprised to find that no cars were allowed in.

"What's going on?" I asked.

"They're going to pave the roads here tomorrow. That's why no cars are let in. It's about time. The potholes."

He was distracted while he was talking to me. I interviewed him quickly and was on my way. He stopped me at the front steps and said, "Just a minute."

He took a small cactus from off the ledge of the window.

"There were babies," he said. "I'd like you to have this. I know you like them."

He walked out with me as I thanked him. He showed me the side garden again.

"I'm just going to cut it back so it will grow thicker next year," he said.

When I got home I realized I had forgotten to ask him one important question. I was busy the next day so I went back on the weekend.

I was shocked at what I saw. Pebbles were scattered on the road covered by a watery black liquid. The road hadn't been graded and, it either sloped at the sides or was all wobbly. I rang the bell at number ten. There was no answer.

As I was certain he was there, I rang again. While waiting for him to answer, I looked at the side garden expecting to see the usual delight. Instead, blobs of uneven tarmac covered everything.

I rang again and he slowly opened the door. He shuffled through the sun porch and looked at me with a deep sadness. I didn't know what to say. I followed him inside to the kitchen.

"You'll help me," he said. "I can't do it myself."

"Of course." I said. But I didn't know what he meant.

He took a geranium off the kitchen windowsill.

He seemed unsteady as we walked out into the garden. His arm shook as he placed the little pot on top of the tarmac.

"I'll start again. I'm well used to that now. I will start again."

The little pink geranium looked small against the scarred black ground – a timid blush of hope under the hot sun.

SUNFLOWERS

Matilde was painting in the kitchen when Philippe arrived. Her latest work was a shock of reds, oranges and golds. Autumn colours, thought Philippe. He didn't pretend to understand her work, though he liked it.

"I am just finishing up. The children are in the living room doing homework." Matilde blew him a kiss.

Philippe heard them from the hallway. They were definitely not doing their homework. It was a game they often played when they were indoors too long. A simple game. Simon would tickle Anick until she had had enough. Her sign for that was, "I just can't stand it!" Then Simon would stop and they would laugh together. Philippe heard the phrase just before he entered the living room.

"What did you say?" he said loudly.

"I just can't stand it!" they chimed together and ran to him for hugs.

"I was told that you two were doing your homework." He smiled at them. "Hurry now and finish before dinner."

Philippe went into the study, sat in the comfortable leather chair and put on some classical music. Berlioz this time. It took away the frustrations of work. He imagined all the unpleasant things in his life simply wafting out the window, carried by these strains of music.

Matilde called everyone to dinner. Her painting was put away, the table was set and the food was ready to be eaten. This was a special time for the family as they recounted their day in a more amusing way than it had really been, shared observations and told jokes. Matilde was excited to be part of a group exhibition in October.

A loud knock at the door made them jump. Since they had a doorbell, a knock was not expected. Matilde opened the door cautiously onto two policemen with grim features.

"Good evening Madame," one of them said. "We have a report that there may be a child in distress here on these premises."

"I'm sorry but you must have the wrong address. There are no children in distress here."

Matilde went to close the door but the officer pushed his body in so the door wouldn't close.

"We take every call about child abuse very seriously. Are there children on the premises.?"

"Yes, but only my own children. And they are fine."

"We have to check everything out very thoroughly."

"They're having their dinner. I'll call them."

"We would rather look around. Step aside please, Madame."

Philippe couldn't hear who was at the door and he was making the children guess who it was. They were not prepared, though, when the two large policemen walked into the kitchen. Matilde followed behind and gestured towards the table.

"My husband Philippe.....and these are our children, Anick and Simon.

The policeman looked around at the dining scene. One of them asked the children where they went to school.

"You can tell us if there is something wrong. Anything weird. Anything. We're here to help. Nothing to be afraid of."

The dog, Sullivan, shoved its nose into the leg of one of the policemen for a pat.

"Well," said Simon, "Yesterday, Maman collected us from school and we walked home through the park. This man's dog did a big poo on the sidewalk, and the man just walked on. We had to clean it up."

"Yes," said Anick. She made a face. "It was so disgusting."

"Yes, I'm sure it was. But I want to know if you feel ok here."

They both looked up at the policemen.

"But of course," said Simon. "It is our home."

"And you, little girl?"

"I feel very well here. It's a lot better than school."

Matilde accompanied the policemen to the door. When she came back, they all looked at each other in confusion. Then Philippe began to laugh.

"I just can't stand it!" he whispered. "That was it. It was the tickling game!"

The next day Philippe was still laughing at the incident at dinner when the present, suddenly and uncomfortably, made itself known. Phillipe jammed his crotch into the turnstyle and a light flashed red.

"Damn!" He had forgotten his ID card again. A security guard approached and told Philippe to accompany him to the security office while someone on his floor was called to come down to vouch for him.

"But you know me. We've been through this before. I've worked here for seven years."

"So you know the procedure."

He heard the click clack of high heels on the stone floor and turned to see the grim face of his supervisor. Manon Bedard was fashionably dressed and immaculately groomed, and would have been absolutely stunning, except for her angry eyes and impatient manner.

"For Christ sakes Savard. This is the fourth time this month. I'm on a schedule and you're wasting your time, and mine."

"Well, this is completely unnecessary. I don't know why we need so much security just to go to work."

"Say that when a terrorist gets in and blows us all up."

The woman quickly signed Philippe in, walked away towards the turn-styles and disappeared into an elevator. Philippe signed for his guest ID pass and followed suit. The elevator eased up to the 23rd floor where Phillipe deposited himself in his office. Later at a meeting Ms. Bedard handed out agendas. The last item called for distribution of more work among the employees.

"But this is Denise's file. Where is she?" Fanny was a strong-minded woman, originally from Haiti.

"Denise will be off for several months. Doctor's certificate. Nerves. Nervous breakdown supposedly."

Manon looked annoyed. "So we'll all have to share some of her work."

"But that's the third person off with nerves. It's not fair to load all their work on us."

"The work has to be done."

"Thank God," Fanny whispered to Philippe, "I only have five years to my retirement."

Back in front of his computer screen, he thought of a song. It was about ancestors. It told the story of how a French colonist on the St. Lawrence, delighted to have a bit of land in the new world, struggled to clear that land so that his children could have a future. Then on to the next generations where sacrifices were made and improvements were made to the farm. The story ended with the farm being sold by someone in this last generation who moved to the city to become a civil servant. "That's my story", thought Philippe.

An alarm broke his reverie. Fanny was trained in emergency measures and she herded them to a side door. They had to wait for a signal and then walk calmly down the stairs and exit in a straight line. Being on the 23rd floor, they had to wait until the other floors cleared. At least Denise wasn't there. She had claustrophobia and always panicked in the narrow stairwell with so many people in front and behind her. When they eventually got outside, it was almost time to go back in again. Fire drills! To his horror, Philippe discovered that his guest ID was in the pocket of the coat left upstairs in his haste. Ah well, it was almost time to go home anyway.

It started to rain as Philippe was halfway through the park. He saw Simon and Anick when he turned into his street. They were wearing their rain gear and were walking Sullivan. He watched them stomp in puddles and open their little mouths wide to catch raindrops on their tongues. Matilde had taught them how to catch snowflakes in winter. A gift from the sky she would say.

The children suddenly noticed him. With broad smiles they ran to him, their mouths still open.

"Papá, you do it too. It's a gift from the sky."

Philippe put his briefcase down on the wet ground. He looked up at the damp sky and stuck out his tongue, letting the cool drops refresh his mouth. Then the dog shook off water onto them all. Laughing and wet, they ran towards the house.

Once the children were in bed, Matilde mentioned an email she had received from the owners of the cottage they rented every year in the the Gaspésie. The cottage had been sold and the owners were moving to Florida.

Matilde smoothed back Philippe's hair. "It's ok. Well find somewhere else. As it happens, an artist friend of mine is going away for a couple of weeks this summer and is looking for someone to look after her place. She lives on a farm up north."

"What kind of farm?"

"She grows sunflowers. And ... she paints sunflowers."

Holiday time finally came around. Sunflowers it was! With the car packed up and ready to go, they headed north. The route became more and more forested the farther they travelled and the children dozed off, lulled by images of countless evergreens. Suddenly they came to a large group of dead trees, grey and solemn – some with bare branches reaching up to the sky in eerie silhouette, others with rusty needles still clinging.

"Oh, dear," said Matilde. "What happened to the trees?"

"I know from my summers working in the woods when I was in college that's something tiny with a ferocious appetite."

"What?"

"Spruce budworm. A golden wiggly thing."

"That's terrible. Those trees are completely dead."

"Don't worry. The government is controlling them with a spraying programme. You saw that small airport back a bit with the yellow planes?"

"Yes."

"Well, it's there just for that reason."

The farmhouse was a centuries-old stone dwelling. Matilde's friend had furnished it in the old style as well, with lots of pine, woven rugs and earthenware pots. The lake was in front, and behind was a sea of yellow, the sunflower field. Beyond that, an open meadow, which led onto the forest.

They swam, canoed or kayaked on the lake in the mornings or went for long walks. In the afternoon Matilde painted in preparation for her exhibition and Philippe read. He had brought a good supply of books he hadn't had time to read during the year. He enjoyed being disconnected – no internet, no TV. After dinner they would play games or talk about when Matilde and Philippe were little, or remember past holidays.

Simon and Anick were playing hide and seek among the sunflowers. Anick didn't like it there. The leaves scratched her bare arms and legs and she got lost among the tall stocks. Simon told her that sunflowers were really big bugs with malevolent eyes watching all the time. Scaring even himself, Simon took Anick's hand and led her to the meadow.

Philippe put down his book. The sun was shining on the lake, moving with it in small ripples. He walked around to the back of the house and watched the dog bound after the children through the sunflowers and across the meadow, edging the forest. A slight smile crossed his lips.

Anick was twirling like a whirling dervish and Simon was circling the little girl. They were laughing. God knows what game they were playing! Then they stopped and looked up at the sky, their little mouths open. Philippe was puzzled. Were they trying to catch? Sunbeams? The blue sky was only marred by a whisper of cloud. What were they doing?

Just then a small yellow plane came into sight, spraying the meadow and the adjoining spruce forest over and over again.

Philippe, horrified, ran towards them as they stood, mouths open in bliss, Simon calling ... "Gifts from the sky, gifts from the sky".

NAMING A CABIN
IN CANADA

It was almost like starting over. There were no broken appliances. No clutter. No dampness. Actually, there was nothing at all. It is surprising how attractive an empty house can be. We stood there in the afternoon autumn sunlight that streamed in through the window, tinted by warm oranges and reds of the leaves. As we stood with arms around each other's waists, we did not imagine what it would look like with furniture. We only felt the space, free for a while, all the objects in our other home fading to unimportance.

What we took for silence was in reality the sound of the wind in the trees, the raucous call of a crow or a jay, the sweet song of a chickadee, and although we didn't want to fill our little cabin with things just yet, we did want to name it. We didn't want to put up a flag as we thought that it would be too bold a gesture, but because you were Irish and I was Irish three generations back, and Irish again when I married you, we wanted an Irish name.

We got the feel of the cabin itself, the sense of old wood. The smell of it. The clean, dry walls. The pretty windows. The closed-in porch for sitting out on summer nights away from mosquitoes. A name signified staking our claim in the midst of third and fourth generation Scots. They were nice neighbours. They came over and sat with us on the floor and told us about the people who lived in the cabin before us for generations and had in fact built the place with their bare hands, clearing the land beforehand. A fiddler, James, had lived in our cabin and, many's the time the furniture was piled out in the porch so that people could dance.

"The piano was against that wall," someone said.

"His wife used to play."

They tapped on the hardwood floor. "This is the original."

The dances were eventually moved to the Women's Institute Hall because more space was needed. The dances proved to be so popular, that people from other villages would come for miles to attend.

We had found a name, we thought. We would call the house in Gaelic after the fiddler that lived in it –

Teach

Tigh

Teach,

Tigh,

Teach an Fhidiléara,

Tigh an Fhidiléara.

No, the sound wasn't right.

Teach an Fhidíl.

Perhaps! But not quite there.

With no curtains, the outside blended with the inside. There were trees everywhere: deciduous ones wearing their bright autumn colours, a dark forest of spruce, pine and fir almost surrounding the house on three sides. We were told the forest was so deep you had to be careful when walking there. You could get disorientated and lose your way in an instant, never to be seen again. We had discovered one danger on our own. Walking in the early morning sunshine, our reveries were broken by the sound of gunshot. We had forgotten it was partridge hunting season, had not even worn red, or was it orange you were supposed to wear?

It was nice to think that bears, foxes, porcupines, skunks and moose made the forest their home. That's what we could call our house – Teach an Choille, house of the forest – but we discarded the idea, deciding that the forest was better left to the animals. It was too wild. Although, walking along a path one day, we came to a place under the trees where someone had dumped several old beaten up trucks. They had their own charm, rusted with weeds and trees growing though them. A wasps' nest nestled inside the engine of one of the weather-beaten vehicles.

As the days went by we explored a little further. A few minutes down a dirt road was an old wooden wharf that had seen better days. Small fishing boats bobbed in the water alongside. Lobster traps, now that the season was over, were piled to one side waiting to be taken to a place of storage. The beach was rocky but there was a thin stretch of sand near the wharf. Eel grass grew up in the sea, making us edgy when swimming. What moved amongst the seaweed?

Eel grass. Feamainn, Teach, House of the Seaweed, Tígh na Mhara, House of the Sea.

A man came to the house selling blueberries. He said his name was Moses and that he was from the Mi'kmaq reserve at the point at the end of the shore road. He told us words they shouted to the packs of dogs when they got out of hand. We pictured the words phonetically:

Gig-il-aie Go away, Kus-a-muk Go home, Men-tu Devil

"Ah, useful," we said. "But tell us something nice."

"Well-eg-is-gu-ge, it's a beautiful day." "Up-na-moo-gess, see you later."

We drove slowly on the potholed roads around the reserve and saw the shabby houses and the packs of strange-shaped mongrels roaming the area. The human factor contrasted sharply with the beauty of the point where herons waded in the blue grey water that stretched into a sky of the same colour tinged with pink. Fir trees lined the far shore, lined up like Christmas trees waiting for decoration.

"Well-eg-is-gu-ge," you said.

"Yes, it is a beautiful day," I replied.

We were relieved to turn off the rough road onto the highway. Because it was a rented car, we took more risks but we didn't want to break down. In fact we were on our way to town to buy supplies. The nearest place was an Acadian French village.

"I know," you said, "why don't we call the cabin Chez Malloy?"

"What's wrong with Chez Conneelly?" For I had kept my maiden name.

"It sounds a bit too posh for a cabin. It would better suit a French Restaurant."

As soon as I said it, a sign loomed on the right saying Chez Maurice, advertising seafood, fruits de mer.

We did our shopping and checked out the restaurant on the way back. Fried oysters with chips and coleslaw. Cold beer.

It was dark by the time we got back to the cabin. Outside on the deck we found a plate of brownies and other sweet squares, a present from one of the neighbours. We didn't know which one or if we had even met them. We would ask around and find the right person to thank. We had no telephone so we would have to call on people.

Even after a big meal we managed to wolf down a few pieces of the sweets. The sugar was comforting and gave us energy to go out and walk along the dark road. There were no streetlights. A fox trotted out of the ditch, through our yard into the woods. Something was making riots of noise from a pond through trees somewhere off the side of the road. As we walked hand and hand we looked up. What seemed liked thousands of stars hovered in an inky sky, almost close enough to touch.

Teach an Rialta, Tigh na spear, Rialta geal ag titum

And then cuddled up in our sleeping bags, we listened to night sounds and the creaks and cracks of the cabin.

"Come here to me, you."

"Who are you calling you?"

"Come here to me then, Treena?"

The air in the cabin was nippy without heat. There was a fireplace in the living room but we had not yet arranged to get some firewood. We joined up our sleeping bags and inaugurated our new summer home, snuggling after, feeling each other's chests rise and fall with breath. We were almost asleep when I jumped up tripping in the bedclothes.

"My God, Brian. There's a fire over there in the corner. Something's burning. We have to put it out or we'll be torched."

I could see you looking at me strangely. Just as quickly as it had jumped into life, the fire had faded to nothing.

"I don't see or smell anything," you said.

"It's gone. It must have been a trick of the light or something." I couldn't stop staring at the spot that was lit up a moment ago.

"It seemed so real. I thought we were gonners."

The next morning we drove to Laurel Goudin's farm to order a cord of firewood. He said he'd heard that we had no furniture and was wondering how we were able to sleep there at all.

"It wasn't so bad," I said. "But I had this nightmare. There was this enormous fire in the corner of the room."

Laurel tapped his pipe on a log, lit it and put it in his mouth.

"You know what they call that house."

"No, we don't," we said in unison.

"Maison Brulée."

We exchanged a look.

"Way back in 1850, there was a dispute between two neighbours over a woman who had come from England to stay with her aunt. Women weren't exactly plentiful here at that time. There was fierce competition for this girl's hand. Finally she agreed to marry the man who lived where your cabin stands and they moved there together after the wedding ceremony. But the neighbour was completely smitten and took the marriage hard. With the attitude of 'If I can't have her, he won't either', he set fire to the cabin while the husband was in town for supplies. The cabin, with the young wife inside, burned to the ground. The site remained vacant for a long time as the grieving husband moved away. One of his nephews built the cabin you are now in."

"It seems like such a happy place."

"I'm sure it does. And it was. There were great people after that who led long contented lives."

We were quiet on the way back to the cabin. The idea of naming our house lost some of its enthusiasm. With the news of the sad history, we examined the cabin again but found nothing but peace and calm.

A white van pulled up outside the back door. And a man in high rubber boots got out. We greeted him at the door.

"I have some lovely mussels, clams, crab and mackerel. Five dollars a bag."

"No lobster?" you asked.

"Not in season."

We settled on some clams that we planned to cook with pasta. The fisherman threw in a few mackerel.

"I heard there are strangers living here."

"No. There are no strangers here. Only us."

He nodded, a perplexed look on his face.

It was only when he left, and we were back in the cabin, that I began to laugh.

"What's so funny?" you asked.

"Just listen to yourself. Your accent! We are the strangers, the foreigners they are talking about."

And we had our name. We went the next day to a man who worked in wrought iron and ordered a sign that said "Áit na Strainséirí", place of the strangers. It had a nice ring to it.

SOLVING THE LANGUAGE QUESTION

Chantal scanned the bus. She usually grabbed a place by the window and put down her bags next to her so she wouldn't have to sit beside anyone. However, there was only one seat left, next to a businessman by the window, his briefcase beside him.

"Is there anyone sitting here?" asked Chantal. "Je peux?"

The man only nodded and cleared his things. Chantal couldn't be sure if he spoke English or French. She put the shopping bags with the new clothes she bought in Montreal in the rack above her seat. Then she took off her new mohair hat and scarf, stuffing it in the sleeve of her coat. Sitting down, she pulled the coat over her like a blanket. Once out of the city the leaves shone in autumn colours until the sky turned a nasty shade of grey and large drops started to fall, first in large splotches and then as a continuous stream. Chantal's eyes started to get heavy and she looked distractedly at the businessman. He was young, what her friend Pierrette would call a young executive. Not her type, he was nonetheless quite handsome. It was his grooming

31

that made an impression. His well-cut suit was without a wrinkle or spot. Clean-shaven, his hair was just long enough to look stylish while short enough to give off a serious air.

It had been wonderful in Montreal. Chantal wondered why she didn't move back there. It was not that Toronto was a bad place to live. Her colleagues did their best to include her in social activities: quiet dinner parties, barbeques, wine and cheese evenings. Her work was also satisfying. However, she realised that she felt more comfortable in Montreal. She loved the avant-garde theatres, the off the track restaurants, the elegance of women, the lively intellectualism of men. A gross generalization she knew, the exact same things could be found in Toronto if she took the time to look. And it was not as if Montreal was without its share of sleaze. Toronto had caught up with Montreal in terms of sophistication and amenities. Montreal had just been there first.

Strange this competition between cities. Spain had it too. Chantal had recently spent a couple of months in Barcelona doing research. The city always boasted it was the cultural centre of the country with new theatres, exquisite design and great cuisine. Madrid, although the political capital, was always the land-locked shabbier cousin.

A language thing again perhaps. Castellano in Madrid and Catalan in Barcelona. English in Toronto and French in Montreal. That was Chantal's line of research: the influence of language on cultural and sociological orders. Hopefully her studies would bring her back to Montreal more often. Now that she had her taste back for the city, she wanted to spend more time there. No reason why not. The college only needed her for a few classes so she could arrange something. The fellowship was for three years. Another two to go. Then she could go where she pleased. Perhaps she'd go further afield: to India or China. Plenty of different languages and dialects there. Or maybe to Japan. Or to Guatemala with its 28 distinct Mayan languages.

The businessman was looking out of the window. Chantal was sure that he could see her reflection but sensed he didn't want to talk. So she joined his gaze into the drizzling darkness. She sighed and let herself drift off to sleep, waking off and on as the bus stopped at lights or slowed down through towns. Once she woke up horrified to find her head leaning on the shoulder of the businessman. She quickly adjusted to a straight position although he didn't appear have minded.

Waking after dozing again, Chantal took a book out of her bag. The businessman was reading some papers, what looked to be a report – French or English, it was hard to tell. She usually knew. He was so clean-cut. Probably English! The French usually had a slight bohemian quality. Then again this man was so good looking and had a certain *je ne sais quoi*. He must be French!

Discreetly straining to look at the papers, she blushed when he moved them away and looked at her suspiciously. Secret business deals no doubt. But then what was he doing on the bus with confidential documents? Breathing in deeply to keep awake, Louise opened her book. Travel always made her sleepy. The book was recommended by someone in the English department at the university after a discussion about living in a place that was not your own.

In English the book resonated with a sense of isolation not only because of the place but of the character bent on self-destruction. She was just beginning to study Spanish but the image in the book of the old horror film posters left a lasting impression on her. *Los manos de Orlac*. She spread her hands in front of her, constricting them into claws. Out of the corner of her eye, she saw the businessman beside her look at her slightly amused. She closed the book and lowered her eyes.

We always go back to our roots thought Chantal. Lowry made the main character in *Under the Volcano* an Englishman and a drinker like himself. He'd had to place it in Mexico to get such powerful images of destruction: the heat, the mangy dogs, the cheap drink, volcanoes ready to erupt. Was Chantal bent on self-destruction too? Away from her roots, was everything a façade? Was her research of any use, or was it just a way to get more letters after her name? *Les Mains de Chantal* She imagined herself in a horror show with her features hideously distorted like those in a house of mirrors.

It was hard putting up with the rain. The journey would have been much more pleasant in sunshine with the air conditioning on. Or even in snow, bright even though the sky was grey. Montreal was a real winter city. Snow piled high, icy winds fingering around skyscrapers. High boots and fur hats. Underground tunnels leading from building to building downtown, from shop to shop.

Mon pays c'est ne pas un pays, c'est la neige. And in France they had called her accent quaint. Just like Gilles

Vigneault. So antiquated! Toronto was more hers than Paris. An icy shiver ran through her before she allowed her eyes to close. She snuggled deeper into her coat. Images of the businessman flooded her. His clean smell and neat appearance.

In her dream she imagined her head falling again against his shoulder, the fine weave of fabric soft against her skin. She could feel him breathing and sense the heat from his hands as he touched her shoulder. Then she remembered it was just a dream. Cars and transport trucks whizzed past, the rain splashing off their wheels.

The bus driver announced that it would be ten minutes before arriving in Toronto. Chantal moved her shoulders. The businessman lifted his head, adjusted his glasses. Chantal stood up and pulled the new pink mohair hat and scarf out of her sleeve. She was dressed to face the bad weather.

When the bus pulled into the station, Chantal got off and walked away. She turned back once and tenderly watched the businessman waiting for a taxi.

"Au revoir," he mouthed. With a smile, she walked into the rain.

CLOTHES HORSE

The sewing machine whirled inside Luigi's studio. He was working on his designs again. I'd told him to create something new but he always thought it was safer to copy. That way he knew which fashions were popular. There was no risk. No great gain either. However, he finally agreed to give it a go. He had seen women's reaction to him when they thought he had created something of his own. There was also the small matter of his mounting debts. He made enough to live on but the payments on the loan for his new sewing machine and other equipment were far behind.

I peeked in the crack of the door. His workshop was more a garage than anything else, a big cement room. Bolts of material added the only colour. I could almost feel the silks, the velvets, the taffetas. He had his head down in concentration so I could only see loose curls on the top of his head. I wanted to ask him if he wanted a break to have a cup of coffee with me but I didn't want to interrupt him. He was finding it hard to do something new, something that was his.

My canvases were drying in my studio upstairs. I always felt they were in a cocoon at this stage. They were never completely done until they dried. Then they could emerge as butterflies or moths, something new anyway, a finished product. I painted in the mornings when the sun was young and full of life. Afternoons were for reflecting and socializing. Since I was finished for the day, I decided to take a walk along the narrow streets with steeples and towers shooting up above terracotta roofs. The earthy hues and curvy lanes were so unlike the straight lines and primary colours of my paintings. Yet they seemed to suit each other. I did not feel out of place here.

Café de Pu was up the hill to the left. It was a steep climb, my exercise for the day. There, a few old men played dominoes in the corner. Television blasted out the latest sporting event above the chatter of voices. As I sat at the bar sipping an espresso with a glass of water on the side, I could see her puffing up the hill. Her weight seemed to fluctuate – up and down, up and down – but she was never really fat. He'd known her for what? Six months?

"Hello Paolo," she said in a loud voice that made the old men stare.

"Hi, Becky," I replied, looking her over.

Luigi was teaching her how to dress. He wouldn't have approved of those shoes with that outfit. Americans want to be comfortable. That always came before style.

"Where's Luigi?" she asked.

"He's in the workshop. He's finally designing a collection of his own," I said.

"That's great. He's so talented." Her voice got even louder with excitement and I cringed a little bit. She used her voice to express herself; never using her hands to make a point or show feeling. Her face appeared blank and wide-eyed without marks of life etched into it. Becky was pretty, beautiful perhaps, but there was no drama in her features. Not an interesting subject to paint. Yet, perhaps with time!

"I'm going home in a few weeks. I want to buy one of your paintings to take with me," she said.

In contrast to her loud voice, I started to whisper. "My paintings are very large."

"I know. It's for my parents. We have a big house." Her eyebrows closed in a frown as if she could not figure out why I was whispering.

I told her to come round to my studio and look at my work. I should have left things as they were but I decided to make a strike for Luigi's future.

"Luigi's talent is wasted," I said.

"Oh, he's not," she said. "He's wonderful."

"I'm not saying he isn't good. I am just saying he hasn't got the exposure yet. All he needs is to get noticed."

"Well, I've told absolutely everyone I know about him. He has got at least ten new clients because of me."

She was getting excited. It's not every day you get a chance to be a saviour. Trying to sound bored and off-hand, I went in for the kill.

"Hasn't your family got a chain of shops across the States?"

She shifted in her stool, started coughing and then sighed heavily.

"Yeah, well, not in all the states. New England," she murmured.

"New England," I repeated, nodding.

"Yeah, New England," she said.

"Well, if you were to bring some of Luigi's designs and show them to the shops, maybe he could get a start. All he needs is a start. I know he has it in him."

Becky blushed and looked down at the comfortable shoes.

"I've never really had anything to do with the stores. My uncles run them. I just get my 25% discount."

"But, I mean, you know the guys at the top."

"Yeah, I know them. They're my uncles. I played with their children every summer. I swam in their pools. But I've never talked to them about business."

"But you could. For Luigi."

She looked at me with horror, and then with resignation.

"Yes, I could." She paused briefly and looked up at me. "For Luigi."

I felt like I had wrung the neck of a dove. Nonetheless I could see this working. It could be the break Luigi needed. Getting into America with his new designs would make all the difference in his career. I'd have to talk with Luigi. He was going about things all the wrong way. Since I had convinced him that Becky was an important contact on his way to fame, he had started pursuing her amorously. That was the wrong approach. Americans preferred to think they discovered genius.

"When are you going home for the summer?" I asked.

"In three weeks."

"You could bring home a collection of clothes to show to your uncles and maybe they could put in an order. If they like them, that is."

"I'm no good at that."

"The clothes will sell themselves."

"But you don't know my family. I don't know what will happen. They fight and complicate things. That's why none of my generation went into the business. That's why I am here."

"If Luigi gets his start, we can afford to all stay here."

She looked as if all the fight had gone out of her.

"I don't want to have to carry too much luggage."

"We'll have it all arranged for you."

Becky pulled herself up straight. I thought she was going to summon the courage to refuse the proposal. But then a smile spread across her face.

"Luigi could come home with me. Everyone would love him. The clothes would sell themselves as you said."

I had to admit that she had a point but I was not ready to relinquish my hold on Luigi and let him wander without me half way across the world. It may very well be the making of his name but it was too soon. His clothes could go and he would stay here. The clothes are enough for now.

It wouldn't be forever. I always knew Luigi would be going his own way. It was just a matter of time. He was becoming popular with the girls. Dressing in his fashions made them feel good. Not long ago it was only I who knew his potential.

But it has been a long time since he's climbed the winding staircase to my bedroom. I took him in when he was a 16-year-old apprentice in Salvatore Senna's factory and set him up in his own workshop. He had been doing a steady business in his own custom ladies clothes – copies of course. It was my idea to start on original designs. Perhaps I should have left him as he was, copying designer fashion, adding little elements of his own.

A few months ago a girl with volatile black eyes and a perfect nose stayed for dinner with us. Her name was Pia. She had been hanging around the workshop a lot. I hardly ever saw Luigi alone anymore.

I arranged all the details with Becky the next day when she visited my studio. She tried to back out but I was hearing none of it. On top of that, I sold her the largest and least attractive of my paintings. It cost her a fortune to have it packaged and posted. I felt a bit sorry for her but not too much. I would be living on the proceeds of that painting all summer.

Luigi was sewing like a maniac to have the collection ready before Becky left. The pile of clothes was rapidly growing. There were brocade jackets, silk dresses, linen suits, suede dresses and matching coats. The designs wouldn't set the world on fire but the material was good and the cut, sewing and tailoring were impeccable. It wasn't long until the collection was ready.

Becky flew to Boston in early summer. She wrote to us about her progress. She held a fashion show for her friends in Boston and ended up selling a few. However, their personal cheques, which she sent along, took three months to clear and a healthy commission was taken by the banks.

41

It left Luigi in debt. Becky was finding it hard-going. There were complaints that there were no labels and that some were wrinkled.

The last letter said that Becky was going to work in Cape Cod for a month and that she was leaving the clothes with her mother to try and market.

When she arrived back here, she had another small personal cheque for Luigi. She said that she'd seen no point in carrying the clothes all the way back to Italy so her mother had held on to the clothes and would still try to sell them. Her uncles had not been interested. "Too European," they said.

"Some start!" Luigi muttered. He held out the cheque she had given him.

"I hope your mother is enjoying my clothes." His eyes narrowed. He tore up the cheque and walked away as Becky looked after him, wondering what she'd done wrong.

I didn't see Becky after that. She kept to herself and didn't go out. She had stopped hanging around Luigi, crossed over to the other side of the street when she saw me and was heard to mutter under her breath about how corrupt Europe was compared to the US. She soon went back to the States, moved to Cape Cod and is apparently living with a family of raccoons.

Luigi moved out of my house, and in with Pia of the black eyes, who had been lurking on the sidelines for a good while. He got his own workshop in town and made a reputation for himself as the best copier of design fashions ever. Everything tailor-made. Haute-couture.

I haven't decided yet what to do with his old workshop. He took all the fabrics with him but still scattered on the floor are remnants of silk, crepe, satin, organza, and other names that conjure up words like drape and rustle and flow. I have made a little collection of cloth and bring it with me up the winding stairs to remind me of him.

PRICKLY BUSINESS

Texas Pete adjusted his cowboy hat as he drove his van down the highway. He pressed a button on his mobile phone that was attached to the dashboard and let it ring ten times before a recorded voice came on and said to leave a message after the beep.

Frowning slightly, he kept one hand on the wheel while he smoothed down his moustache. Loralee had called it droopy to match his bedroom eyes. Although he didn't need to, he leaned slightly forward to speak into the phone.

"Pete here," he said. "I'll have another consignment ready to be delivered next week. Have all the precautions in place. Be in touch later. Bye."

Pete hadn't planned to be on the wrong side of the law. It just worked out that way. A loner, he had quit or had been fired from a number of jobs before he realised that he would be better at running his own business. Now he couldn't do anything else; it was profitable and he loved it.

A sign on the side of the road said that a trucker's diner was coming up soon. Pete indicated and drove his van into the parking lot. It looked small beside the long trucks. Inside, Pete ordered pancakes and sausages with strong coffee.

Waiting for his order, he took out a newspaper and began to read. He was about half way through when he jumped up, bumping into the waitress who was bringing his breakfast. His coffee spilled on her and she hollered. He excused himself but did not offer to help her.

There was a pay phone up by the cash desk. Pete put in his credit card and dialled a number and waited for an answer.

"Did you see the paper?" he asked. "It's too risky to smuggle the merchandise from Mexico anymore. I'll have to pick them up in Texas." He added that the price would have to go up because of the risk.

On the other end of the line, George Spomoni, an east coast businessman, was sitting behind his expensive desk shifting papers from one pile to another.

"I don't care where they come from, as long as you get them. I have clients waiting, he said. George narrowed his forehead. "You have a good reputation as a rustler. I know you will be fair."

"Yeah," said Pete. "But did you see the news about the cowboy that got arrested and sent to prison for smuggling 20,000 in from Mexico?"

"You talk too much," whispered George. "We have a deal. I'll go higher. We'll work it out. "

Pete said that he'd just got a little jittery. The shipment would arrive on schedule and they would negotiate a new price.

"I have to get back to the shop," said George, "Just doing a bit of paper work." He hung up.

The waitress was waiting for Pete to get back to give him a piece of her mind, but Pete just walked out of the diner without even glancing at his breakfast. He got back in his van and started driving again. With the air-conditioning broken, Pete kept lifting off his hat to wipe his brow. Small towns and villages disappeared behind him and a fine dust blew up and coated the van. Pete looked over to the passenger seat to make sure the water cooler was filled.

The desert was home. He liked the challenge, the openness of the land, the little lizards and the loneliness of it all.

Pete drove off the main road onto a side road leading off into the wilderness. After an hour, he parked and took out some rope from the back of the van. A herd of cattle stood grazing in the distance. Pete looked at the animals distractedly while he took out spade and put on gloves and a protective leather apron.

Walking over to a cactus, Pete dug it up, carried it over to the van, lifted it in the back and covered it with a tarpaulin. He repeated the procedure until the van was full, occasionally taking a break for water and to look over his shoulder.

***

The New York florist was full of roses, lilies and other heavenly scented blooms. Potted trees of every kind lined the back wall. A well-dressed woman was admiring a large cactus.

"How much is that?" she asked.

The shop owner, Mr. George Spumoni, shook his head.

46

"That one's not for sale."

He told the woman how scarce cacti were becoming; popular indoors and out because they required very little care. Now, because of that, there were all sorts of new laws to protect them in their own habitat.

"But we're getting in a consignment later this week," he added. "For special clients that is. Very hush-hush".

For a minute George thought the woman looked shocked, but in a low voice she said, "I'll take ten."

BULLFIGHTER

The studio manager signalled that there were three minutes to go on *The Living Daylight* Show with PJ McKearnan. PJ was seated beside another suited man on a Current Affairs set, the interview in progress. Then the sound faded and the musical theme came on. PJ sat still and looked at the camera until the music finished.

"…and out," said Joe, the station manager. "Good one PJ. The last eh? For a while anyway."

PJ stood up, thanked his guest and walked over to the studio manager who was standing by the camera.

"That's right Joe," he said.

Joe slapped him on the back.

"I'll see you at the pub in a few minutes. You can't leave without having a few pints."

PJ nodded.

"OK so. I'll see you there," he said.

When PJ entered the pub, Joe was already in the corner talking to Nadine, who had just started as a production assistant at the station. Other colleagues were chatting at the bar.

Joe called him over.

"Hello PJ. There you are. We were wondering where you'd got to. You know Nadine?"

PJ looked at her intensely. And with his smooth number five broadcasting voice, he said. "Not nearly enough. A shame I won't get to work closer with you."

"Perhaps you will."

"No, Nadine, my dear, it is my last night."

"What do you mean? Are you leaving?"

"I've rented a cottage on an island off Donegal for a year. Going to write. Always wanted to write."

"But you're coming back then?"

"No, I don't think so."

Joe patted him on the back. "Sure, you won't be able to get on without us. You'll go mad there, and be on the show again in no time."

PJ shook his head.

"Well, what are you having?" asked Joe.

"A pint of Guinness. "

"Right you are. And Nadine?"

"Oh, a vodka lemon. Thanks". And when Joe left she turned to PJ.

"I always wanted to get into TV. I don't understand. You'd quit a good job to do nothing."

"Absolutely!" he said understanding Nadine's horror. He knew what it was like to try to break into the media world, to be obsessed. He had thrived on it for years. Now he was glad to be leaving it.

"Aren't you a little old for that sort of thing?" she asked playfully, stretching her long youthful legs.

49

"Going away to find yourself and all that?"

"Despite what you think, I still have all my own teeth. I swear. Never too late to change. New horizons. That sort of thing. "

"I didn't mean…but an island. For a social animal like yourself? You have quite a reputation."

"Well, yes, I know. But there are other sides to me too. I have this book I want to write and since I'm free now …"

"Yes, well, I heard about your marriage last year. Sorry."

"Just one of those things. It had run its course."

Nadine excused herself to go to the toilet while Joe arrived with the drinks.

"Are you going after that young one? She's a cracker."

"I like her. She has something. Any good as a PA?"

"Still learning the ropes. But has potential. Has potential."

Nadine came back and took up her drink.

"You know. I've always wanted to live on an island. Sort of romantic."

PJ leaned closer to her. "Well, my dear Nadine, you have an open invitation. The only one I'll allow on my island."

***

The wind never stopped. It pummelled the rocks and swept across the island from various directions. The old cottage, however, was comfortable inside with wooden beams and a fire blazing in the large stone fireplace. PJ sat in an armchair surrounded by crates of old books and notebooks. The nearby table was piled with papers and a laptop. PJ had been reading his old diaries. In his hand was a large notebook with a brocade cover of red and gold. The diary he was reading was from the time he had just finished college and gone to Spain. One page had an ink drawing of a bull charging a bullfighter. The handwriting underneath said March 18, 1986.

"Here I am in Madrid. My Spanish is not so bad now. I met a few bullfighters. They think I am mad. I haven't had the courage to ask them to teach me yet. I know I am meant to be a bullfighter, only born in the wrong place."

It was strange to read about his younger self, the past flashing before his eyes. What kind of a creature was he to think that a young Irishman with no experience could become a bullfighter. What was the attraction anyway? The danger? The clothes? The cheers?

***

After several months, PJ was walking on the beach, the wind attacking his hair. Looking out to sea, he took his jacket from his shoulders, held it like a bullfighter's cape and swept it. He had to fight against the force of the wind to keep it in the right position. Images and words from his youth in Spain came back to him.

"Myself against sheer animal energy and strength. A girl throwing down carnations, smiling at me."

He'd read the passage in his diary that afternoon. He should have been writing the book instead of wallowing in the past. But something compelled him to keep re-reading the old journals. Perhaps that girl, Nadine, had been right. It was too isolated. He was lonely, and felt he was slowly going mad.

The cheers of the bullring in his head mixed with the pounding of the surf. PJ thought he saw a girl dressed in a red and white flamenco dress walking up the beach towards him. He was indeed going mad! He shook his head but the girl waved and called to him. He responded by giving the jacket another shake and sweep, playing along with the dream. The flamenco girl called again, but it had turned into Nadine from the TV station, dressed in jeans and a T-shirt.

"Is it you?" he asked.

"You said I was the only one invited on your island. No warning, I'm afraid. No telephone. No email. What have you been doing with yourself? You must be demented."

PJ put out his hand to feel that she was real and brought her into the kitchen of the cottage to warm up after the island wind.

Over cups of tea, Nadine looked him over.

"You're different," she said. "I think you've been alone too long."

"And why do you say that?" PJ asked.

She put her cup down on the table.

"Your hair is standing up on end and you have a mad look in your eye," she answered.

PJ put his hand on his head to smooth his hair.

"Have you got much of the book done? How can you fill your time?" Nadine asked.

"Just reading," he replied.

After supper, PJ poured two glasses of whiskey and they settled down front of the turf fire in the living room.

Nadine looked at the piles of books on the table and in crates. Lifting one out of the box, she held it up.

"What are these?" she asked.

"Just old diaries," PJ replied.

Nadine shook her head. "That's not healthy."

PJ defended himself. "I suppose it's something I have to do," he said.

Nadine started silently reading the book she had picked up, and then giggling, she read aloud with an American Southern accent.

"I'll just die if I don't get in a bull ring," she read.

Nadine put the book down.

"Don't laugh at me, Nadine. We all have dreams and obsessions when we're young."

PJ realised how he had missed the company of another person. He and Nadine explored the island and had long talks together as they climbed over the rough rocks. Nadine questioned PJ relentlessly on the book he has planned to write.

"I want to see some of it down on paper," she told him.

***

The night of the full moon, they built a bonfire on the beach. Sparks flew up into the dark sky as if they were baby stars. PJ and Nadine sat in front of the fire passing a bottle of wine back and forth, the crate of diaries on the sand next to them. Nadine leaned on his shoulder and whispered something to him.

Standing up purposely, PJ pulled Nadine to her feet. Each one reached into the crate and picked up a diary. Taking turns opening one, they randomly picked out a line to recite and then, with a flourish, tossed the book in the fire.

"*This world is here to distract us. It is not real*," Nadine read before howling with laughter. She threw the diary into the fire.

Then it was PJ's turn.

"*Luz, all the lights of Castille call your name, my black-eyed senorita*".

PJ didn't have to read. He knew it all by heart, saying the sentence with passion, not taking his eyes off Nadine. With a lot of drama and exaggeration, he threw the diary into the flames.

"Into the fire you go, to light up the sky, my little Luz," he said.

Nadine responded with: "*But the bull ended up chasing me.*"

Diary after diary went into the fire until they both huddled closer to read from the last book.

"*I was never so scared*," read PJ.

"*Everyone could tell*," Nadine read mockingly. "*I was so embarrassed.*"

PJ read the next line. "*I'll never go into a bullring again*," he said, throwing the book dramatically into the fire. Nadine laughed as PJ looked down on the empty crate; all the diaries had been burned.

"Hold on there," he said, "that's me you're laughing at, a younger me, but me all the same."

Nadine stopped laughing. "You're right. Sorry PJ," she said.

They turned to look out on the dark sea. Behind Nadine, PJ slipped his jacket off his shoulders and waved it like a bullfighter's cape reacting to an imaginary bull.

"Olé," he mouthed, winking at the stars.

He moved closer to Nadine, put the jacket over her shoulders and kept his arm around her. They stood together lost in their own thoughts, listening to the waves crashing on the night shore until the fire burned down and they felt the horns of cold wind on their skin.

"I'll start on the book tomorrow," he said.

WINE-STAINED

I sat on my grandfather's knee listening to another story about when he was in Argentina. I was beginning to think that he made those stories up. I was almost sure there weren't any kangaroos in that part of the world. Picking up the old man's hand, I absentmindedly started to trace the lines on the palm. They were great stories nonetheless. Grandfather was always in peril and managed to get himself out of trouble at the last moment. He always ended by giving me a whisker rub and a flip upside down. I tumbled laughing on the grass.

"There, Sport."

My hand reached again for his large one. Again I turned it over and put mine close to it.

"Grandfather, why is your hand that colour?" I asked.

"That's another story. That would be the time when the Dapperdy twins held my hand down on a red hot skillet until it sizzled like a slab of bacon."

'Tell me that story," I begged.

"No, that will have to wait for another time. Off you go now and play," he said as he went into the house. I could see him through the screen door as he picked up the newspaper. No sense asking him again I thought as I kicked at a stone in the grass. Once the newspaper was out, games were over.

I went around to the back of the house to the little clump of poplar trees I called a forest. Acting out my grandfather's latest adventures, I fought off a notorious horse thief who almost got away with an entire herd of precious Argentinian black beauties whose wild manes whipped as they galloped hard together across the dry pampas.

Grandfather said that a cousin my age would be coming in a few weeks. In the meantime my uncles and my grandfather alternated between spoiling me and leaving me alone for playtime. They told me to be back for supper; I could do what I wanted until then. This took getting used to although they seemed to think this was normal. I wondered if my mother knew.

It was also ok to talk to strangers here. Grandad said they wouldn't be strangers here, but friends in no time at all. So, people would stop me and say: "My, my, and who do you belong to?"

I didn't understand what they meant for a long time and would answer: "Myself" or "God" or "I don't belong to anybody."

There were those who asked, "Where did you come from?"

To which I replied: "From my mother's tummy" or "from my grandfather's house" depending on my mood. All the old men or women seemed nice enough. I just couldn't understand why they asked me those questions.

Then, one day I was with my uncle Pat when a wrinkled man patted my head and asked: "And where did this young fellow come from?"

My uncle looked down at me, smiled and said : "This is Mona's youngster".

"I might have known," said the old man. "He's the spit of her."

After that, when they asked me that question, I answered: "I am Mona's young fellow" or "I am Mona's boy."

"Mona Dalton?" sometimes they would ask. I would say yes even though I knew my mother's last name was the same as mine. They seemed to get confused if I said it wasn't Mona Dalton. Anyway, Grandfather and my uncles were all Daltons and I supposed I was a Dalton here too.

One of the old men stopped me one day and introduced me to some others: "This is Donald Dalton's little grandson."

One day my uncle Paul took me to the wharf. I couldn't swim yet but I would go down the ladder and paddle about a bit without letting go. I liked the smell of tar, the boats and the big swells of the waves. I was fascinated by Uncle Paul's famous trick. He would stand high up on a post used to tie boats, light a cigarette and turn it around so the lit part was inside his mouth. Then he would dive into the water. I watched as he hit the water and went far under, his bathing suit slipping down from the impact. Then up, a tug at the bathing suit, the cigarette taken out of the mouth as he climbed up the ladder onto the wharf again, blowing out smoke with a flourish to show the cigarette was still lit. He was a hero then. I looked at him holding the cigarette dramatically. The palm of his right hand also had a burgundy tinge.

"Uncle Paul, why is your hand red?"

He looked down at his hand.

"All Dalton's have hands like that."

I thought for a while. My grandfather had a reddish hand. My uncle Paul had a red hand and I was almost sure that my other uncles would also have red hands.

"My mother doesn't have one."

"It's only the men."

"I don't have a red hand."

"Give yourself time son. You have to grow up first. Sure, you're a Dalton through and through. Just look at you." Paul started to tickle my belly. "Your blue eyes, your straight black hair, your freckles."

"My mother has red hair!"

"Red hair, red hands, what's the difference?" Paul picked me up. "She, like you, is a real Dalton even though you have a different name. And as true a Dalton, you must be a strong swimmer."

With that he tossed me over the edge of the wharf. I streaked through the air into the water so deep I feared I would hit bottom. I felt a chill as it got colder the further down I went. I didn't know what to do, so I did nothing, and eventually I started to come up again.

The waves were carrying me back and forth in a rocking motion. I blinked water from my eyes and saw that my uncle was at the bottom of the ladder with his hand outstretched, but I was still far out.

"Swim, Cahill," Uncle Paul shouted.

I moved my hands in front of me. I was doing a dog paddle, but I didn't know that. I only knew that I was staying up in the water, and I was getting closer to the ladder. When I was near enough, Uncle Paul grabbed me and pulled me in. Once up safely on the wharf, Paul held one arm up and proclaimed: "Another Dalton swimmer."

The next day Grandfather was about to tell me the story of the deplorable twins frying his hand in an attempt to find out where he had hidden a treasure-map. I interrupted him.

"I know that's just a story. Uncle Paul told me the truth."

"He did, eh. And what exactly did he tell you?"

"He said that it was a sign that you were a Dalton."

Grandfather looked surprised. "And he's right, of course." He lowered his chin and chuckled to himself. "I'll just tell you the story anyway. Once upon a time I lived in Argentina with my pet kangaroo, Gara. It was a wild place then, and we were there to clean it up ... "

I was becoming a strong swimmer. I was in the water at least once a day. When no one had time to take me to the wharf, I went off the shore stepping carefully over the sharp stones and shells. I didn't need anyone to take me swimming from the beach. I could do that alone.

I was just about to wade into the water when my uncle Peter called me to jump in the car. We were going to the wharf. We arrived just as a boat was coming in. We watched it as it came along the L side and was tied to one of the poles that Uncle Paul used to jump off of. Big boxes of fish were loaded onto the wharf.

"Do you have any spare mackerel?" Uncle Peter inquired. The fisherman gestured to the crates.

"Just help yourself," he said. Here's a bag."

Peter helped himself to six good mackerel. He put his hand in his trouser pocket to pay the fisherman but the man stopped him.

"Put that away now."

Peter thanked the man and picked up the bag. I was about to turn towards the ladder and go for a swim when my uncle made a big gesture over me and said: 'Have you ever seen an eel Cahill?"

I looked back and saw what looked like a slimy, slippery snake wiggling in my uncle's hand. I ran as fast as I could to dodge the eel. Peter got tired of chasing me and finally threw it at me. I jumped off the wharf to avoid it, but got hit in the middle of my back. I turned in mid-air to see uncle Peter. His red hand was outstretched.

It wasn't as much a shock hitting the water this time. I had done it before and had time to close my mouth and eyes as I plunged deep into the dark grayish-green water. When I surfaced, I could hear my uncle shouting.

"That's the lad. You jump off the wharf just like a Dalton. There's good blood in you, eh?"

From then on I only used the ladder to come up. There was no hesitation when I jumped. It was if I had always jumped off the wharf.

Neither Grandfather nor the uncles cooked or cleaned. They had hired a woman called Darla who did all the chores. Grandmother stayed in town and only came the occasional weekend. Darla was a motherly woman with a big bosom. Someone said she had almost become a nun, but left the convent just before taking her final vows. She loved to hug and kiss me but I thought I was too big for that. After dinner, Darla cleaned up while the men stayed around the large dining room table. Grandad would go to the cupboard and bring out the bottle with the two little Scottie dogs on it – one black, one white.

This was another time of the day that I was left to my own resources. Sometimes I was content just to sit there and listen to the adult talk, and at others I drew or played with the toys I had brought.

Uncle Peter was the youngest brother. Some said he was the best looking. He liked to tease Darla and would grab her around the waist and then push away from her in a dance, his arm stretched out. His hand glowed red.

It was Darla who put me to bed when she had finished with the kitchen. One day she left early and no one remembered to put me to bed. I woke up in the middle of the night curled up in the big armchair in the living room with all my clothes on.

***

I was getting excited as the cousin they had mentioned was coming soon. Uncle Peter was driving into town to pick him up at the train station. The boy had his own little room on the train so he could lie in bed and watch everything go by.

"Do you want to come, Cahill?" Uncle Peter asked.

I nodded. Peter then lifted me in the jeep, as the step was too high. We drove through wooded areas dotted with clusters of houses along the road.

"Jamie is exactly the same age as you. He's your second cousin once removed. Do you know what that is?"

I shook my head.

"Well, he's the son of your mother's first cousin."

I didn't even know what a first cousin was. It didn't matter as long as this boy liked to play in the woods, swim in the sea and pick berries. I could share secrets with him. We stood together on the platform as a whistle announced the arrival. People moved off the train in ones and twos. The conductor lifted a boy down. He waved at Uncle Peter who put out his hand to shake with the boy just like adults. a red hand clasping a pale one. Then I was introduced to Jamie. We didn't shake hands; we just looked each other over.

Jamie had straight light brown hair and blue eyes. He was shorter than me and had perhaps a more delicate frame. We went back to the cottage as soon as Peter stopped for something for his sailboat. He promised us a sail on the weekend. Jamie turned out to love all the things that I loved to do but it was even better because he had been there before. He knew what gardens to rob, where caves were, hidden places and secrets in general. I asked Jamie if he heard about the red hand of the Daltons. He had. He flattened his palm.

"Our part of the family doesn't have it."

"I'll get mine when I'm older," I said confidently.

"I know, why don't we make our hands red now?" Jamie pulled me over to Peter's boat shed. Normally it was locked but we just undid the latch and we were inside.

"Even if it was locked,' said Jamie, "I know where the key is hidden."

63

The boat was standing on a frame in the middle of the shed. It had been freshly painted a gleaming white. On the bow the letters t-h-e-space-r were painted in red paint. Uncle Peter planned to call the boat 'The Ruby Sea". Paint cans were piled neatly over to one corner. We took out a red one and pried it open.

"Go on Cahill,' said Jamie.

I opened my fingers and placed my hand gently on the surface of the paint. I then lifted my hand up and turned it around so the paint wouldn't drip. Jamie started to do the same when the door of the shed opened and Uncle Peter came bounding in.

"Caught you red-handed."

His face was like the sea during a storm. I backed away from him and tripped over the leg of the frame. I put my hand back to steady myself. The colour of Peter's face was getting a darker red and I thought he might explode. I was ready for a shout of anger but Uncle Peter exhaled in a big hearty laugh. He pointed to the boat. Against the white hull was the shape of my hand in red paint.

"I was looking to change the name anyway. I'll have to call her The Red Hand now. You'll have to help me get her ready and in the water before I take you for a sail," he grunted.

We worked hard every day, mostly fetching, holding and lifting things but we learned a lot about boats. My uncle let me paint on the name using stencils. On the Saturday a man arrived to help launch the boat in the water.

The Red Hand was a small boat, but it handled well. Uncle Peter issued orders that we followed. We worked hard but enjoyed the feeling of adventure, the salt air and the feel of the cold sea as it sprayed up over the decks. If we had been inside the cabin, we would have been seasick as the waves picked the boat up and slammed it down over and over again.

We were in our bathing suits and were shivering. Uncle Peter couldn't leave the tiller, but he motioned for us to lift up one of the seats. There was a bottle of whisky with the Scotty dogs on it. He motioned for us to take a drink out of the bottle. Jamie went first, and made a face as he passed the bottle to me. The whisky went down easy enough but then I felt a warm, burning sensation all through me. The waves were getting wilder. The boat leaned so far to the side that we thought water would flood in.

Uncle Peter managed to turn her just in time. Through the rain, mist and high waves, a tugboat could be seen. It was a rescue boat from the shore. We climbed aboard as the tugboat captain tried to make himself heard above the wind.

"The old man's gone," he said.

We read his lips more than heard his words and still we didn't understand what he was actually saying. He must have realized by our expressions that we were still in the dark.

"Donald Dalton had a heart attack. Your father died this afternoon," he shouted to Peter.

He patted my uncle on the shoulder and then helped him attach the sailboat to the larger boat. They left the little sailboat to be hauled behind. I was given a cup of hot tea. Uncle Peter splashed some of the contents of the Scotty dog bottle into it.

"That'll warm you up," he said.

Darla had warm clothes and a wood fire warming the living room. My eyes started to close as I sat wrapped in a woollen blanket in front of the fire. My uncles were going up to town and Darla would stay at the cottage with Jamie and me.

The next morning we dressed in our Sunday best. An old man picked us up and drove us the 28 miles to town. I greeted my uncles and my mother as I walked through the door of my grandfather's large house. A few people were milling around the living room.

The casket was in the corner near the grandfather clock. That seemed appropriate somehow. Looking down on that pale face, I had trouble feeling that it was the man who told me stories. I wanted the to hear those stories again. His hands were folded together, intertwined with rosary beads. I touched them and then tried to gently pry them apart and over so I could see the palm. There was a soft tap on my shoulder. I turned around to find an old man with glasses. I didn't remember him from the beach cottage.

"What are you doing?"

"I am Mona Dalton's young fellow." I said, quickly dropping the hands of the corpse.

"This is my grandfather. Someone told me that a red palm was the sign of the Dalton family. I was just trying to see if it was still there after he died."

"Do you have the red hand, son?"

I hung my head. "No I don't."

"That's good for you."

"But I will have it when I am bigger," I protested.

The man gave a short laugh.

"I'm your grandfather's business partner and friend. I've known him all his life. I have my own silly theory about that red hand, and I know his sons have it too."

"What's that?"

"I know it makes no scientific sense. I loved your grandfather and I love this family."

He winked at me.

"But to tell you the truth I think they've been a bit too fond of the drink."

I opened my palm and looked down at it as if seeing it for the first time. My mother caught my eye from across the room and smiled.

PEARLS

Penny was five years old when Kitty McCabe built a house next to hers. Kitty had grown up in the town and had come back to retire. Age had smoothed its hand over her face, pressing wrinkles into her skin and adding little hairs on her chin. It could not, however, take away her sense of style or the fact that she was still attractive and well-groomed. Penny remembered the fur coat falling off the woman's shoulders in winter and the broad hat and pearls in summer. Those pearls were a part of Kitty McCabe as much as anyone could remember. They would loop loosely around her neck twice; the individual beads, about the size of a large pea, gave off a subtle lustre. She always held a cigarette holder, although she seldom smoked.

The house was much grander than Penny's. It was not that it was a lot bigger but it used space well, was more modern. They lived a few miles out of town along the river. Modest homes were scattered among the trees on the riverbank, so when Kitty bought the old school house and started doing it up, it caused a stir.

First of all, she had all the outside plaster taken off, baring the stone underneath. At the back of the house facing the river, she had two enormous picture windows installed. Downstairs was basically one big room with wooden floors and a kitchen, laundry room and bathroom to one side. There were two bedrooms upstairs with high ceilings. Part of the attic was closed off for storage and accessible only with a ladder through a square in the ceiling.

The most unusual part of the house was a glass conservatory at the side. People said it would break from the weight of the snow in winter, but it didn't. Kitty loved her house. She had retired early from nursing in the city. This was at a time when few women worked at all. She didn't have a family to look after, and seemed to have so many interests. The conservatory was full of plants and herbs.

Binoculars and a book on birds of Canada were always handy to be able to identify the feathered creatures that frequented her feeders. Books about flowers and art were in a small bookcase over to the corner. Artist supplies for watercolours and painting on silk were on the bottom shelf. Stylish people went in and out to visit or to play bridge and even dance.

As next-door neighbours, Penny's family kept an eye on Kitty since she lived alone. Her mother went in every day to see if she needed anything. Sometimes she stayed longer than usual and, seeing that the young girl was getting restless, Kitty would take her up to the spare bedroom and let her play dress-up with some old clothes and jewellery. She liked the nurse's cape the best. It was dark navy blue, lined in red with two golden lions as clasps. Kitty said she had worn it during the war.

"Are you a nurse?" Penny asked.

"I am," she said. "but I don't work now. I was in a hospital in the city for a long time. Before that was the war. That's when I wore the cape."

Kitty looked into space for a moment, then sighed, and left Penny to her game. Penny pretended to be Supergirl, the cape blowing behind as she flew into the air to save someone. She soon had a game for each item of clothes. She went to balls in long dresses. She went to work in an office in the tweed jackets. She was a teacher in the wool dresses. She was a queen, a fairy, an actress. Each game would be embellished so that it became quite an intricate piece of theatre.

One day Kitty was returning from the hairdresser's with her short white hair done in soft curls. She looked at Penny and said: "I know you!"

"Yes," the girl said, "yes, you do."

She nodded seriously and went into her house. Shortly after that the neighbours began receiving the phone calls. Miss McCabe had forgotten her handbag in the shop. Miss McCabe had missed an appointment. Miss McCabe gave a $100 tip to the newspaper boy. Miss McCabe should not be driving. She drove too slowly and would cause an accident.

Then, she did cause an accident. She just stopped in the middle of the road to look in the mirror to put her lipstick on. She was fine but had caused several cars to bump into each other. The police told her not to drive any more. Penny's mother did her shopping and organised for her to be taken out for a drive once and awhile.

One night they could see smoke coming from her kitchen. Nora Black, Penny's mother, had a spare key to her house in case Kitty locked herself out. She used it to let herself in. There was a pot burning on the stove. With a cloth, Nora took it off and put it into water at the sink. She turned off the stove. Penny wasn't allowed in because the smoke was thick, but she heard what had happened. Nora rushed from the kitchen to look for Kitty. She was sitting in an armchair looking out the big window out at the lights shining from across the river.

"Kitty, what are you doing?" cried Nora. "Did you not see the smoke?"

Kitty just continued to look out the window.

"Mother, let me ... My baby ... I want ..."

Nora left her with her thoughts and went to the kitchen to make her a cup of tea and some toast. This town fed distress. As a result, there was more than a fair share of overweight souls.

The toast was ready. Nora brought it in, and sat with Kitty. She felt there was no point in telling her that she had no baby, that she had never married and that her own mother was long gone. She stayed until Kitty's head fell and a slight snoring could be heard. Then she covered her and left.

Kitty had always been so independent. Imagine nursing in the war when she had barely left home! However, it was obvious that Kitty could not cope on her own any more.

Nora spent most of each day with Kitty after the fire and then she phoned Kitty's relatives. She had many nieces and nephews; a few still lived in the area. They were always good to Kitty and visited quite often, but as they didn't live beside her, they didn't realize how confused she had been getting lately. Nora reached Carl who was a great organiser. He had always arranged for the snow to be cleared from the driveway, for a gardener to come in summer and for spring-cleaning to be done. Birch logs were delivered each autumn on his request and someone was sent for repairs whenever they were needed.

"She can't be that bad, Nora. I was in a few weeks ago and she was fine."

Carl didn't want to believe that there was a problem but he had to admit that he had been getting phone calls about problems his aunt had been causing.

"I guess we should have someone with her. You couldn't do it, Nora? You know her as well as anyone."

"I'd like to Carl but I have my own family to look after. I don't mind looking in on Kitty. In fact, I'd like to. But she's going to need someone full time. I can't be away from my own crowd that long."

"Well, it's going to take a while to get things organised. I have to find someone, talk to Kitty and talk to her lawyer. Could you stay with her until we find someone else?"

Nora agreed to stay with her temporarily. Kitty was difficult because she wanted to go out, but she couldn't find the car keys, which had been hidden from her. Frustrated she called a taxi, saying she wanted to get her hair done. No one could stop her.

Penny played pirate in the woods beside her house until dinner was ready. They were having fish cakes, her favourite. They had just sat down to dinner when they heard a commotion out in the driveway. A taxi was parked there. Kitty was still in the back seat and the driver seemed to be arguing with her. Penny had never seen Kitty anything but composed, but she was visibly upset. Nora went outside and took Kitty by the arm, got the key out of her purse, brought her in and sat her down in front of the big window. Then she went out to see the driver again.

"I'm sorry but I just didn't understand the woman." he said. "First she asked me for some address that's not around here, and got quite upset when I told her I didn't know where it was."

He brushed his hair back with his fingers.

"I went to ask the hairdresser what to do and she gave me this address. She said the other one was her old city house. The lady kept saying we had to pick up her baby. It was fine until we got here and then she wanted to pay me with this."

He showed us a playing card, the ten of hearts.

"She insisted that this was $10. She even told me to keep the change. I wouldn't mind but I've got a family to feed."

Nora told him she would pay the fare if he gave her a proper receipt.

Kitty looked out the window at the lush riverbank, the powerful river with its irregular undulations, a pretty little wood to one side and Penny's house to the other. The sun was beginning to set and painted the sky with pinks, greys and mauves. Soon it would disappear and the dark night would cough up stars or perhaps an orangey moon. Maybe there would only be a black sky. It was always so dark. There were no streetlights here. But Kitty was not there. She was away in France. What she looked out on was a flat area full of lingering smoke and scarred by artillery tracks. The Canadians had just captured Vimy Ridge from the Germans.

***

Kitty was in the makeshift hospital working round the clock to save the great number of wounded. Since Kitty was one of the few nurses who had experience in surgery, she worked hand and hand with Dr. Davey. The blood and pain were overwhelming. Most of the soldiers were just her age or younger. They were far from home and some would never make it back again. Her good sense of humour sustained her, cheered up her patients, and kept the surgeon going.

"Wipe those specks off your face nurse. Oh, I'm sorry. I forgot. They're freckles," the doctor teased over and over again.

When they had finished operating for the day, Brad would help her clean and sterilize the equipment and get the operating room ready for the next day. Then they would walk out in the fields and pretend there were no trenches, no gas to change the colours of light, no ugly wires winding like thorns. They looked up at the sky and talked about home, a home that presented very different pictures to each of them.

For Kitty it was the crashing of the sea, the V formation of wild ducks, strands of seaweed with its pungent life-giving odour. For him, it was the hard, dominating feel of the Rockies, solid and powerful in the distance. They talked about the wildness, the crispness of an autumn in the woods, the brightness of fresh snow. Faces came and went. Images of mothers, school friends and small town characters were mixed with smiles, tears and screams of some of the patients they had attended. When things were particularly bad, another difference became apparent. The young doctor quoted from the Bible while Kitty moved her fingers nimbly along a long string of beads.

***

Preparations were now being made for the sitter to move in to look after Kitty. Drawers and closets in the spare room were cleared out. The boxes of old clothes were given to Penny so she could continue to play dress up. She took them home, cleared out the toy box in her room and started putting them all in there. She eyed the navy nurse's cape, the delicate party dresses, the well-made work clothes, straw hats, fur hats and little ropes of fur that looked like a small animal was biting its tail. There were lacy nightgowns and silky scarves. Mixed among the clothes was a bag of the old beads and pieces of jewellery Penny also used to play with. She found a special box for these, added what bits her mother had given to her and kept it in the toy chest along with the clothes. She fingered the dangling earrings, jingled the clunky bracelets, and hung the beads over the top of the chest.

Lorraine Sutton moved into the house the following week. She wasn't a nurse but was able to cook and care for Kitty, keep an eye on her, and call for help if she needed it. Kitty didn't like her at first but gradually grew more and more dependent on her. Sometimes Kitty implied that someone was after her rings. Then she accused Lorraine of hurting her. The sitter got very upset and threatened to leave but, with a lot of convincing, she agreed to stay. When things were really bad, Nora stood in so that Lorraine could have a little time to herself.

The doctor came and went. Kitty's heart was getting frailer by the day. She wouldn't take the tablets as she imagined that someone was poisoning her.

Lorraine got used to Kitty's strange utterances.

"What have I got in my hand?" asked Kitty teasingly.

"Let me guess," said Lorraine, "is it an apple?"

Kitty didn't answer. She was back with Doctor Davey as they played a game to make them feel closer to home.

"Guess what I have in my hand? We have them at home." said Kitty teasingly.

"I'll describe it. It's flat and slightly smaller than my hand. It has veins going through it and can be different colours, depending. It can be soft and smooth or so dry it crumbles to dust."

"Is it alive?"

"Yes."

"Then it's easy". He broke into a smile and backed away. "It's you!"

"Silly."

Kitty shouted and chased after him. It was so dark that they toppled into a huge hole, laughing.

"You don't act like a doctor at all."

"Oh, don't I now.' He held her shoulders, bent closer and kissed her.

"Now, I'm not acting like a doctor at all."

They were full of mud when they made it back to the clinic.

"What was the object I was supposed to guess?"

"What do you think it was?" She wasn't giving anything away.

"Time is passing so quickly. It seems like yesterday since we arrived here." Kitty agreed.

Several months later Kitty searched Brad's face while he was reading an official looking letter.

"What is it?"

He pushed her gently and knelt in front of her while looking in her eyes.

"They're sending some of these boys home, and you are going with them."

She could hardly believe the good news.

"And you?"

"I'm going to stay a few months longer here, and then go to England for a bit."

Kitty cast her eyes down and Brad took his hand in hers.

"There will be some things waiting for you from me when you get back home to Canada. They have been in our family for years. I want you to have them and I hope that someday you will join our family. I love you Kitty."

A smile crept on to his face as he teased:

"How can I go without those lovely freckles?"

***

A nurse was coming once a week. Kitty had fallen asleep in a chair, and had fallen out of it, breaking her leg and her wrist. Penny went in to see her with Nora. She seemed to be in pain. She moaned and shouted "No" loudly. She didn't talk to anyone anymore. She was lost inside her head and the words she uttered were in that context. People felt embarrassed, as if they were listening in to something that wasn't meant for them. They turned away and talked among themselves and let Kitty stay with her own thoughts.

***

The trip home to Canada from the front was long and difficult. The wounded and recovering were transferred in large transports to the nearest port, across the English channel and after a brief rest, back to a ship. The freighter left as soon as the men were loaded on to it. The cold North Atlantic was rough and dangerous from storms and enemy vessels. Kitty had to fight seasickness thorughout the long voyage to Montreal – it took them over a month. There was a doctor on board, but she was the only nurse. Those who didn't make it were bundled up and buried at sea. Kitty thought that this was better than being left underground in a strange land. The sea was somewhat more universal.

In Montreal, Kitty stayed with her patients for another month. It was felt that a familiar face, with some knowledge of what the men had been through over in Europe, would do the men good. During that time, the war finally ended and the morale of her patients shot up. There was a lot of help and Kitty could relax more. However, she still felt seasick. Her legs felt wobbly and she often had to run to the toilet to throw up.

After the month, Kitty was given permission to go home to the east on leave. There she would rest for a few months until Autumn, when she would go back to Montreal to nurse at the city hospital. She'd had her medical. She had packed, and before taking the evening train, she went into the men's ward to say goodbye. Those who could, started a slow clapping sound. Most looked visibly emotional. Kelly hobbled towards her; his left pyjama bottom pinned up just below the knee. He handed her a card and a small packet. She had to reach for her handkerchief to whip tears away while her fingers tore at the paper. It was a bottle of French perfume.

Dr. Galloway came in the door and told Kitty to see him before she left. Kitty said her goodbyes. She had spent a great deal of her time with these men. Kitty left her luggage by the front door and went up to the second floor and knocked on Dr. Galloway's door. He called for her to come in and smiled at her when she did.

"I have several matters to discuss with you. You have plenty of time before your train leaves. Anxious to get home again, eh?"

"Yes, Doctor," she replied. "It's been a long time."

"I'll agree with you there. I want to commend you on your service overseas. You have a real way with those men. Must be that eastern charm. You make them feel there's still something to live for. Half the battle, I always say."

"Thank you Doctor," she said.

The doctor shrugged. He opened his desk drawer and took out a slender box and placed it on his desk.

"These were sent by my good friend, Dr. Kelvin Davey. Apparently his son Brad got word to him to say that he had fallen in love, and wanted the girl to have the Davey pearls. They've been in the family for generations. I've known Brad since he was a baby. He was an only child, a fine chap and very good doctor. I trained him myself. Anyway, his father sent these to give to you."

Dr. Galloway slid the box across his desk. Kitty took it tentatively and opened it. The most beautiful pearls she had ever seen lay coiled on blue velvet lining. She took them in her hand, feeling the smoothness of the beads with her finger. She put them on. They hung long and heavy, so she looped them several times around her neck. They were exquisite.

"Now, about your medical ..."

Kitty was late and almost missed the train. She had booked a compartment and sat inside looking out the window smoking.

"First call for the dinner," she heard a male voice calling up and down the corridors. Normally she would make her way down to the dining car. There was always someone from home on the train to let her catch up on the news, but she didn't feel like meeting anyone now. The familiar landscape, so often dreamed about in France and in England, whipped by. These long strips of farms, these gentle trees and waterways of Quebec had been exactly what she wanted to show Brad when he arrived back in Canada.

"Second call for dinner," she heard.

It was not worth torturing herself over that now. Dr. Galloway had ended everything. Why had he given her the pearls when he knew it was for nothing? She had wanted to return them, but he insisted she keep them. The Medical Officer had continued to be kind and fatherly when he gave her the bad news that she was pregnant. He passed her a report and a letter to give to her local doctor. He told her that, although he felt a loyalty to inform his friend Kelvin Davey, she was a nice girl who got carried away being so far away from home serving her country. It wouldn't be going on her military record. Then he took her hand.

"It would never have worked, Kitty."

She hardly listened.

"The religion difference is too strong. Your family is well-respected but there's too much of a bridge to cross. Better to stay apart".

"Last call for dinner. Last call," The carriages rattled loudly as they swayed along the track. When the porter came in to make up her bed, Kitty was surprised at the darkness outside the train window. She managed to laugh at the porter's jokes but when he left, she sat on the bed and fingered the pearls at her neck as the impact of what Dr. Galloway said set in. Would she never see Brad again? No, he would come for her, love her again.

The train edged into Lévis, where it always stopped for refuelling. A full moon sat on top of the Chateau Frontenac, poised on the cliff across the wide St. Lawrence. She had always looked forward to this scene but now turned away. It was bitterly romantic.

Her hometown wiped all the bad news of the past day away, along with all the horror of the war. It looked just the same as she had left it, quiet with people slowly going about their business. Down the hill from the station wooden houses dotted tree-lined streets that led down to the river. Her father came to meet her, smaller than she remembered, but dressed impeccably in black. His usual reserve disappeared when he saw her, and he broke into a smile.

Her mother met her at the door of the house, told her that her trunk would be brought up to her bedroom later, and asked if she wanted to freshen up.

"The peonies are in full bloom," she said. "Light pink and dark rich wine ones. The smell is heavenly."

As Kitty walked out to the garden, she thought of how big the house was now that all her siblings had left to form families of their own. The house would have made a great hospital. She shook her head. The war is over.

At first her mother tried to get Kitty to rest, whether because of the war or because, through women's intuition, she suspected something. However, as time went on, she tried to involve Kitty in volunteer work, in welcoming men home from overseas and helping the local doctor. While Kitty waited and waited for Brad to come and take her away, she found it pleasant to have her parents to herself. It was also comforting to be back in the place she had grown up. But she knew it could not last. She couldn't go to her post in Montreal in her condition so, giving up hope that Brad was coming, she contacted a friend working in an orphanage in Montreal and was hired on as a nursing sister. She crossed fingers that they would be able to help her.

"You've changed, Kitty. You are more grown up," her mother remarked at the train station en route to Montreal. "I used to worry that you'd be all alone in life. But now I think you are fine just the way you are."

Kitty hugged her before steeping up on the train. Her trunk had been checked in the baggage compartment and she carried a small bag with just the essentials for travelling.

***

"Dad. Forgive me," cried Kitty, whose mind was deteriorating rapidly.

Lorraine didn't mind. She was strong and could lift her. Didn't care if her mind wandered. Lorraine had her own fantasies, along with a big supply of movie magazines.

***

Kitty arrived at her new position. MacDonald Orphanage turned out to be a well-run affair. The children were well fed, cleanly-dressed and treated fairly. They loved their new roly-poly nurse. Experienced in soothing the men in the war, Kitty was able to help some children cope with their loneliness, and teach them to appreciate the life that was in front of them. Kitty was getting bigger by the month but no one seemed to notice. Her friend Julie knew, of course, and was sure that she would be able to deliver it when the time came. What better place than an orphanage for it to happen!

Kitty kept her spirits up, although secretly she was disappointed that Brad didn't come and find her. She decided she would try to live a good life, and if she couldn't be with the man she loved, she would be an eccentric old lady living for the day. Sitting in her room with her single bed, a wardrobe, a chair, small table and her trunk covered with a blanket for a bench, Kitty kept dreaming up scenes in the future for herself. She did this in order not to go crazy. Brad featured in her dreams, less and less as time went by.

Just after Christmas, Kitty started to feel unwell and have severe pains.

"It's too early," Julie said. "There should be another two months. That's if everything is okay."

"It's not okay," Kitty snapped. "I know the baby's dead."

Julie said that they should get the doctor, but Kitty made her swear not to.

"We can manage it ourselves. We went through the war," she said. 'This should be easy."

It wasn't easy but Julie made excuses that Kitty had stomach flu. She got others to take on her duties as she looked after her friend. Julie begged Kitty, who was bathed in sweat, to take off her strand of pearls but she refused. Clutching on to them, she gave birth to a little boy, still and dead. Julie handed the child to her after she had cleaned him up. Kitty rubbed the cold face and gently kissed it, as if that would bring him back to life. It was not like death, not like the death she had seen in the war, painful, gory and lonely. This death was peaceful.

"What's going to happen to him?" she asked.

She cradled and rocked the little bundle back and forth, touched his little hands and feet.

"They're usually put in the furnace," Julie replied.

'What if I were married?' she asked.

'Same thing." Julie shrugged failing to see the distress in Kitty's eyes.

At that point, the bell rang for mass. Julie said that she had to run, but would be back to check in on Kitty and take care of the body.

Kitty looked down on the innocent form and decided he was not going into the fire. She would have to work fast. Calling up energy she didn't have, she got an extra pillow and several pillowcases from the wardrobe She had smuggled them in case her linen was ruined in childbirth. She placed the small form on the pillow, gently kissed its little lips and encased it in several pillowcases. Then she put it all in her trunk and recovered it with the blanket.

Despite her weakness, she went down to the bathroom for a shower and changed into a clean nightgown before Julie came back.

Julie looked around. "Where is he?"

"I took care of it. I placed him in the furnace myself, with love."

Then the tears started. Julie went over to the bed and comforted her. She saw no reason not to believe her. Nor did anyone think anything was odd later when Kitty sent her trunk up to the attic, with the excuse that she wanted more

85

room to put in a writing desk.

***

"Time for your pill, Miss McCabe," said Lorraine, trying to get her attention. She brushed her hair and got her into a clean nightgown.

"I don't want to take that," Kitty protested.

"Come on now, Miss McCabe. The doctor's coming. I have to get you ready."

Kitty fingered her pearls and then touched her hair to make sure it was soft and well-groomed. Accepting Lorraine's offer of a shawl, as bed jackets were for old ladies, she waited for the doctor to come. Dr. Moore was the only person Kitty talked to anymore.

Not many doctors made house calls anymore but Dr. Moore made an exception for Kitty. The old lady was interesting. Perhaps eccentric was the word, but for such an age, she had never given up on life. He admitted that he did flirt with her a bit to break the ice. Knowing he was attractive, Dr. Moore did the best he could to accentuate his good looks. His teeth were white, hair cut the perfect length, fingernails manicured and clothes casual but expensively cut. He had worked on his personality, had just the right bedtime manner, knowing how to flatter his patients and pick out their interests.

He took Kitty's pulse and blood pressure and gave Lorraine another prescription for heart pills. When he left Kitty smiled.

"He asked me to marry him, you know," she told Lorraine. "I would have too, but the religious difference was too strong."

"That's too bad dear," Lorraine said, patting her hands.

***

Kitty didn't stay long in the orphanage. She got a job in paediatrics in the Montreal hospital where she was before the war. She had a nice apartment, a good life with close friends. Never marrying, she worked on becoming the eccentric she had promised herself to be when Brad failed to come for her. Always wearing those pearls!

One year she was invited to march in a big Armistice Day ceremony in Ottawa. A roll call of First World War dead was called out as veterans marched. Then she heard his name: Bradley Davey, Canadian Army Medical Corps. She felt weak and would have stumbled to the ground if it weren't for another woman marcher who held her up. So, he hadn't made it home. He had loved her!

***

Lorraine picked up the ring that had fallen from her slim, delicate fingers. Kitty rocked an empty blanket in her arms.

"My baby," she smiled. "I didn't name him."

And with a sigh she was gone. Her heart had just stopped. Lorraine lay her on the sofa and called her relatives. They came, and after paying respects to Kitty, began looking for her pearls.

"She never went anywhere without them," one of them said.

However, the beads seemed to have disappeared.

Everyone remembered the chain of rich lustre around the neck of their great Aunt, so much a part of her. They spilt up and looked through drawers, in jars, behind furniture. No luck. Someone suggested they look in the attic. It was piled with boxes. The trunk under the eaves was locked. Not knowing where the key was, they got a screwdriver and pried open the lock. All that was in it was an old pillow. Someone picked it up and put it on the floor in case there was something under it. Nothing. As one of them lifted the pillow to replace it, a muted tinkle sounded. He pulled off the pillowcase, and then another, and there, cushioned amongst the soft feathery padding lay a small delicate skeleton with bones of pearly white. All of them stood in silence. Then one of them lifted it, put it back in the trunk and closed the lid. As they filed out the door they noticed the little neighbour girl sitting in the driveway on her tricycle.

'Hello Penny, they said. 'What are you doing?"

'Playing," she replied.

Someone patted her on the head. Penny knew Kitty was gone but, with no real concept of death, she didn't know where.

"I'm in the war like Kitty," she replied, the old nurse's cape blowing behind her in the wind, a flouncy hat on her head, and a string of beads wrapped several times around her neck.

COLOURS OF AUTUMN

They'd cancelled Halloween at the last moment, a big thing for the small town, as it had always been a special night in the area. Firecrackers and caps usually went off two months earlier. Old tires, bits of wood, cardboard boxes, and anything else that burned were secreted away for bonfires. Soap was prepared to mark the windows of stingy residents. Costumes were planned, pranks and tricks practised. On the night revellers usually blocked the roads in and out of the town; this year it was the police.

It was Clayton's fault, of course. They wanted him. They thought he was going to kill some child, some kid dressed up as a bunny rabbit or an angel. Murder capital of the country! Thanks to him the town had become famous. People say he never hurt anyone who didn't deserve it; they had all done him an injustice.

He was now hiding in the back woods, and police hadn't a hope of finding him. You see, he planned well. He had a brain. He killed Father Brannigan, and that woman that worked at the cinema, Annie Moore. Crazy old bat! That was different. They didn't understand him, tried to change him. What right did they have to judge? It was them, not him, that were bad. To make amends, blood had to flow. It wasn't easy. They put up a fight.

He would not be the only one wearing a mask tonight. People wouldn't be able to resist getting dressed up. The little kids were all at the community centre this year. They were going to have sweets and games. The radio told them not to go on the streets, or around to the houses for trick or treats. But some of the older ones would be out. It was in their blood. This was a wild place. Halloween was sacred here.

What did they think he'd do? Burst into the community centre and massacre everyone? Stab everyone he saw in the streets? They'd made him into a monster. But he just did what had to be done.

The last of the autumn leaves clung to the trees, and it was already cold. There were a few snowflakes. He was near the golf course, a place he always loved. The trees were particularly colourful this year. He had sometimes come here to walk; there were other lovely spots around too, but this was his favourite. The members of the club didn't deserve it. He'd watched them, and all they were interested in was getting the ball into a little hole before the other guy beat them to it. They didn't even look at the trees or hear the birds. That's why it was so easy for him to hide. People just didn't see.

There was a light through the trees. It was from the house of that artist fellow. There was an art group over at the community centre once. Clayton had brought in his drawings. The teacher said they were good but disturbing. Disturbing, eh? People needed to be woken up.

It was a risk coming out tonight but there was something he had to do. A lady journalist needed a lesson, and he had a nice surprise for her. It was easy finding out where she lived. That was the great thing about a small town. He had watched her every night for two weeks, but then he'd had to go into the woods to hide.

Flashlights shone through the trees. The sounds of dogs and men filtered through the crisp air.

"The dogs are going mad. He must be near here," someone shouted.

"He wouldn't be as stupid as to come out on this night."

"It is just the kind of thing he would do."

"How are Sam and Joe doing with the roadblock?"

"They're checking everyone coming into town.'

Clayton crossed and re-crossed the stream to put the dogs off the trail. He waited in a ditch and watched the cars after they went through the roadblock. He'd pick one, anyone, and get a lift into town. They would be expecting a guy with long greasy hair. His picture was in all the papers. That woman journalist had called his hair stringy.

With his closely shaven head, clothes that looked like he was one of the searchers and a cardboard sign to stop cars, Clayton watched twelve cars pass and flagged down the next one, saying his car was being used in the search, and that he had to make an urgent telephone call. A young woman was driving. She had a baby in a seat in the back. Though she was very nervous, she let him in, worrying whether to put him in the front or back.

"You can sit up here with me," she said finally.

She put the car into gear and began the short journey into town.

"Why are you going so slow?" Clayton asked.

"If that guy they're searching for jumps out at us, I want to have time to stop. I don't want to have an accident. I don't want anything to happen to my baby. Oh, you forgot to put the lock down on your side."

Clayton was happy to get into town. The woman had been too jumpy; she was making him nervous. She let him off by an old now-disused cinema. He knew a back way in, beside some warehouses. The building was going to be torn down to make way for more offices, for more people with white shirts who didn't have a clue. It was nice as it was at this exact moment. In the darkness, rows of seats were waiting for him to perform, but he wasn't giving a show there now. He walked up the sticky-coated floor of the aisle and sat down on one of the tattered plush seats.

He used to go to the matinee every Saturday. Sometimes there would be a double-bill. His mother would drop him off, and pick him up at the end. Then he would act out the film for her back home, or draw a picture of it. She always said it was really good. He even made up stories for her.

"Your mother's pretty enough to be in the pictures herself," Annie Moore used to say. Same as she used to tell Clayton later that he'd come to no good. When his mother left him with his grandmother and ran off, Annie said that his mother had always been too pretty for this town, too pretty for him.

"It's not easy having a child that demands so much attention," Annie would say.

If he looked straight ahead long enough, he could

almost picture the flickering images of a western movie. When he shut his eyes he could hear voices, music, and clatter of old slapstick comedies. Perhaps he had spent too long in this place as a boy. Time to move now! What he had come for was hidden behind the screen under some old curtain material, just the thing for the lady journalist.

Marie Naughton's house was in darkness except for an eerie orange light from the curled-up smile of a pumpkin looking out of the window from its place on a stand. Clayton went around to the backyard where he could open a window by sliding a knife under the catch. It was easy to climb through. He navigated by touch so as not to turn on a light, his feet making hardly any noise.

The living room was located in the front of the house to the left. She was asleep on the sofa with a baseball bat lying across her stomach. Her hair fell in soft strands over her face: it was a nice colour, golden brown. She looked pretty when she slept, a bit like his mother.

He'd have liked to lie down next to her. Perhaps when this was all over! He put the drawings the art guy had called disturbed under the ashtray on the coffee table. Those were for the newspaper. It was about time his genius was recognized. The other package was for her.

"Surprise, *Little Miss Journalist!* That'll teach you to write those nasty things about me.'

He reached in the bag he had taken from the cinema and pulled out the bony head he'd dug up from her family's grave a few weeks previously. Clayton blew out the candle in the cavity of the pumpkin, put it all in his bag and placed the skull on the table instead. It watched the woman as she slept.

He picked up the bag that now contained the pumpkin, and went out through the back window again. The operation was seamless. If he hadn't wanted her to know he had been in there, she wouldn't have been able to tell. But she'd know! She'd know! A smile curled on his lips as he headed back into the woods to prepare for the day of the dead.

CIRCLES

Molly sometimes wondered what she was doing back in her childhood home again. It was not the break-up with Giorgio, or even the need to get her career on track, it was more of a compelling pull. Molly had to come! She would have come even if the things she used as reasons had not existed.

Her mother, Nell, made her very proud. She had made a life for herself, held down a job, had good neighbours and hardly ever drank now.

Molly, too, quickly found a job in the town but realized immediately that it was a mistake. Her colleagues were into baseball and country music while she liked jazz and intellectual cafes. A chain smoker, she found the smoke-free office hard going and all her continental clothes stuck out a mile among the blue jeans and sweaters. Besides, she just couldn't get interested in reporting on agriculture.

The only thing soothing was the land – the feel, the smell and the sound of it. She bathed in the comfort of it, not daring to be over-enthusiastic about something others took for granted, and even abused.

She didn't put much effort into the new job. It was as if she were waiting for something to happen. All that was needed was to go through the motions until it occurred. And it didn't take long for her to realise why she'd come home. At work, Shelly from Current Affairs told her that some crazy women was on the phone for her. She had a familiar sinking feeling when she took the call.

"I had to call the police," the voice on the phone raved. 'He came to fix the door. I was so shocked. Why would he do that to me?"

Molly thought it was the usual alcohol-induced hysteria of her mother, and didn't try to make sense of what she said.

"Now, Mary's mad at me."

Steve, Mary's son, had been caught at fourteen climbing through windows of a jewellery store for an older gang. Now after five years, he was just starting to get back his reputation by hard work and helpful deeds.

Molly tried phoning the neighbour. Her call was answered, but no one said anything. It was as if the person on the other end wanted to check who was there before answering.

"Hello. This is Molly. I just got a strange phone call from my mother. I was wondering if you knew what was going on?"

She heard a grunt and knew she had got Jim, the eldest brother.

"What the hell is Nell trying to do?"

He was always feisty. Now his anger was overpowering. Molly didn't deal well with anger.

"Steve's gone to get cigarettes for her at all hours. He's carried in the wood. He's fixed everything that's gone wrong in that house. Mum's been Nell's best friend. Even when she was drinking...' He broke off for a few seconds. 'I don't know what she's doing!'

'Calm down, Jim, just tell me what she's done this time? Accused him of stealing or something?"

"Stealing?" he repeated. "Stealing sounds like nothing in comparison."

There was a bang, and then nothing. Her mother had obviously gone too far this time.

Molly spent the rest of the day down in the smoker's room, not contributing anything until it was time to leave work.

The leaves were piled high. She kicked them, hearing them crackle at her touch. "God, had it been right to come back?" she wondered.

The second call came as soon as she arrived home.

"Molly?"

It was an official sounding voice.

"This is Dr. Hill."

'Oh no, she's finally been committed," she thought.

"Your mother is on her way to hospital. I've looked at her x-rays and it's serious."

"X-rays?" questioned Molly.

"Yes. Of the lungs. We've found a spot. We, ah..."

"I'll come," said Molly.

Her mother was strapped to the bed when Molly arrived. She looked tiny but not fragile. Her blue eyes were oversized but not as wild as they usually were when she was in one of her moods.

"They put me in this big hotel. It's very expensive you know. Private room and bath."

Molly listened for a while before going to look for a nurse. Electrolytes, and their imbalance, had caused her odd behaviour.

They sat together everyday, and when Nell's mind became clearer, they laughed when a man caused an explosion in his room by sneaking a cigarette while on oxygen; he wasn't hurt. Molly tied scarves around her mother's balding head, and then when the hair grew back, they giggled because it was a different colour. Her red curls had been replaced by straight, fine, salt and pepper coloured hair. Laughter made it bearable and healed past hurts done to each other. She didn't quite know how to react to what her mother said next.

"The doctors didn't tell me but I know," she said. "I have something growing inside me."

"Yes. I know," said Molly quietly.

"I've always wanted you to have a brother or a sister. I wanted a dark haired girl, and there you were. This baby is going to have hair like me."

Molly held back the tears, thinking about the power of mind and how self-deception can protect us from too much pain.

Nell was allowed to go home after a few weeks. Molly was able to work part-time and hire someone to stay with her mother when she couldn't. She had made a few changes to make the house more comfortable during the long winter. A new hot water tank was installed so they could have as many showers and baths as they liked, and a stereo system was set up.

Molly loved to listen to music and played some to her mother. Nell, she knew, preferred the TV, but listened to please Molly.

Giorgio had been phoning Molly ever since she came back. He sent her cassettes of music and little gifts to keep him in her mind. She had left him, wanted to end everything because she saw no future in the relationship, but she now had to admit that contact with him was one of the things that kept her going. He begged to come across the Atlantic to see her. Nell had met Giorgio once before and did not particularly like him.

"Why don't you find a nice local boy and settle down? There's nothing better than where you're from." she would always tell Molly. But Molly had looked at her mother's loneliness and frustration at living in a small town, and had flown as far away as she could.

Foreign things had always fascinated her. As soon as she learned how to write, she got out Nell's old typewriter and started tapping out requests for information from travel agencies.

"They think you are a businessman. Get as much from them as you can," she laughed.

But Nell changed her tune when she caught a glimpse of the wanderlust in her only daughter's eyes.

Molly associated home with a variety of dogs that had shared her house during her childhood. Prepared to stay around this time for a long time, Molly decided that they should have a dog. There was an advertisement in the paper for puppies. Although they were newly born, and could not be taken away from their mother for another month-and-a-half, she could visit and pick out her little dog. It was grey and black and had just opened its dark eyes for the first time. In her arms, it didn't stop wiggling and wagging its tail.

When Molly returned home, Nell said that they were going to have a visitor. Giorgio phoned to say that he was arriving in a week. Molly expected her mother to be upset but she seemed content. "It will be nice to have a man around the place again," she said.

Molly argued that Giorgio was not the type to fix things in the house. Nell was always going around saying she needed a man, not in a romantic or sexual way, but to fix the broken window, to put up shelves, to catch a mouse.

"That's just sexist. Men are more than stereotypes," Molly would respond, silently hoping for help as she scraped the paint off a chair or tried to handle an unwieldy drill. Nell seemed to want company and a distraction. She didn't mind that Giorgio wasn't the answer to all the things wrong or broken in the house.

Molly got busy. She scrubbed the house from top to bottom, and cleared out two cartloads of unwanted items. As winter was approaching fast, and she knew that Giorgio would be unprepared, she asked her male colleagues at the newspaper if they had any winter clothes they could spare. She was overwhelmed by the response: long underwear, gloves, scarves, mittens, parkas, boots and even ice skates. It was enough to see him through the winter. He just had to take his pick.

The next week Molly hired someone to look after Nell and drove to the city to pick up Giorgio. Was she doing the right thing? Her fluttering heart told her she was, and she felt a pang of regret that Giorgio had missed the leaves in their autumn glory. Those remaining were crumpled brown, lying on the ground or blowing in swirls. Trees that were not evergreens stood bare and cheerless.

The moment she saw Giorgio with his moustache, dark eyes, brown curly hair thinning out at the top, she knew that his visit was the right thing. As expected, he was wearing a thin little jacket and designer Italian shoes, totally unprepared for a Canadian winter. They spent a night in the city before driving back to her mother's house. Nell greeted him in a new nightgown.

As Molly had to work, she counted on old friends to entertain Giorgio. One took him to the cinema, another sorted through the clothes with him and someone else, Adam, asked him to go deer hunting. They started off on their journey when it was still dark and the whole town seemed to be asleep. The side road was lined thickly on either side by evergreens: spruce, white pine, fir, cedar and others. Adam told Giorgio to follow him and found a small path leading into the woods. Giorgio realised that if he became separated from Adam, he may never find his way out of the woods, but wander and wander forever until he collapsed from hunger and exhaustion. Or worse still, a bear, wildcat or one of those moose they'd been talking about, could get him. He looked over his shoulder. Adam showed him tracks in the ground, marks on trees and how to tell the difference between animal droppings. Giorgio asked to see his gun.

"No, I don't shoot anymore. I just track them down to get a look at them. I like being in the woods." Adam perked up his ears. "I used to love hunting. Man against beast. Now, I've lost the appetite for it."

Giorgio lost track of Adam for a few minutes and panicked.

"This country has too many trees," he said.

Back at home Nell was disappointed that Giorgio came home empty-handed.

"I love a good feed of venison," she said.

She went on to say that she loved Giorgio like a son – despite his slightly bald spot.

Giorgio looked for work, needing to contribute financially and keep himself sane. There was absolutely nothing in the area. Young people had known this for generations, and had automatically immigrated to Ontario or 'out west'. He wanted to stay with Molly, but knowing he would have to go, he decided on a compromise.

"I'll go to Montreal for a couple of months to make some money. I'll be in the same country. We can phone each other. There are a lot of Italian restaurants in Montreal."

"But you're an architect," argued Molly.

"I'm Italian first, and I speak French. I'm sure there will be something."

He started getting ready to leave as the first snowflakes appeared in the evening sky. Before he left they went together to pick up the puppy. Later, the dog snuggled next to Giorgio's chest under his coat to keep warm.

***

It was hard for Molly to say good-bye to Giorgio, especially now they had a real feeling of family with the dog and her mother. She found it incredible that she had given him up once before. As his train pulled out of the station, a tear made its way silently down her cheek, hot enough to keep from freezing.

Nell couldn't contain herself.

"My baby has arrived. It looks just like me."

She patted her salt and pepper coloured hair.

Molly took a leave of absence from her job to care for Nell, who was having difficulty keeping her food down and was getting weaker and weaker. It was a two-hour drive to the city hospital where Nell needed treatment once a week, but after a while she refused to go.

"I want to stay home and die in peace," she said.

The dog and Giorgio's phone calls kept Molly going. Giorgio had indeed found a job at an Italian restaurant. Not only that, he had been quickly promoted to manager.

"Imagine, I'd never even boiled an egg in my life before," he told Molly.

"Well, its about time," she joked, trying to hide her exhaustion and desperation from him, as she had with her mother. "Keep cheerful," she kept telling herself.

Months passed. Every week Giorgio phoned. She lived for his stories about the characters in the restaurant, the bums in his rooming house, the concerts he attended.

Christmas was quiet. Nell couldn't eat the dinner Molly had prepared and had not liked her gift. It was a beautiful angel in a large glass ball that snowed gold glitter when it was turned over. Nell dropped it, shattering it to pieces and leaving a puddle of golden sparkles on the floor. Molly thought it was deliberate.

The piles of snow outside her house got higher, icicles grew so long and thick that it seemed that they would never melt. The car had to be plugged in overnight so it could start in the morning. The windshield had to be scraped and the driveway had to be shovelled. The priest, who came to visit every day, said it was a particularly hard winter on the deer.

Molly was unscrewing the top from a bottle of morphine tablets, the strong purple ones, when she saw a drop fall from the bottom of an icicle as it shone in the light of the porch lamp, a first sign of spring. She had just heard the six o'clock evening train go by. A taxi approached. Probably picking up a neighbour she thought as she brought a glass of water to Nell. Her mind was still on neighbours and on how Mary had forgiven them, but had never been as friendly, when the doorbell rang.

Giorgio held out his arms. The dog, remembering him, jumped up.

"I got a real job Molly. I took some time off before I started. I'm an architect again." He shivered. "Will there ever be spring in this blasted country?"

Molly couldn't stop smiling. Even Nell seemed to take a turn for the better.

***

"Whistler" called Molly.

The little grey terrier criss-crossed among the trees

104

leaving a wild pattern of tracks on the snow. As it reached Molly, it jumped up leaving her trouser legs all white and powdery, then took off again. It was one of those crisp days. The sun was shining and the sky was a clear deep blue against a brilliance of the snow. You could hardly see the green of the trees for white but you could smell their freshness. Giorgio found he could see his breath and blew out a few times.

"I discovered this in Montreal," he said. Then he rubbed his arms. The lumberjack-style jacket did a good job keeping him warm but cold air got in through the sleeves.

"We're almost there," Molly said.

They bent down to go under a branch that was lower than usual because of the weight of the snow. All the familiar paths looked different covered in white but she knew instinctively she was going the right way. The trees started to get closer together and the light softened. She sensed the river nearby, silent under its cover of ice. Even Whistler was quiet and stayed close to them.

Molly soon found the first few branches of pussy willows. There was a small clump of them. She stroked the little buds of greyish fluff between her fingers and judged what length to cut them.

"Feel that," she said to Giorgio, and after fingering the buds, he carried the branches that Molly broke off. They walked farther into the woods and found more, breaking off one or two so as not to leave a noticeable scar in the forest. When the bundle was large enough, they started to follow their tracks back out of the woods. Molly turned around and glimpsed Giorgio standing looking down at the pussy willows and she felt such love she thought her heart would break.

A little ball of snow came bounding out from behind a tree. The small black nose peeked out of white whiskers. Little clots of hardened snow hung from its legs. Molly went under the tree branch again to where the snow was lighter and not so hard going. Whistler marked the transition by rolling on its back and making little snorts. Molly watched it for a minute, took the branches from Giorgio and set them down gently on the snow. She pushed him down, rolled him and then joined in.

"Whistler," she said. "Look! We can do that too."

Molly and Giorgio would have liked to have stayed in the woods longer but they had only managed to get someone to stay with Nell for a couple of hours. When they arrived home, there was an ambulance in the driveway.

Father Trainer said that Nell had taken a turn for the worse, but there was nothing they could have done. He offered Molly a lift to the hospital. Giorgio stayed at the house to make sure everything was turned off, and then joined Molly. He left the pussy willows standing in a vase on the window.

Molly nipped down to the hospital cafeteria for coffee as she thought it was going to be a long day. When she came back she saw the expression on the face of the priest standing outside Nell's room. She found Giorgio and buried her face in his chest as she burst into sobs. Molly allowed herself to cry again at the funeral held a few days later. She had been pretending to be cheerful for so long.

Giorgio went back to Montreal to start his new job while Molly stayed behind to tie things up. Then she loaded up her car, set the dog beside her in the front seat, and began the drive through tree-lined roads, now bursting with new growth. Whistler panted at the window, and she remembered how just a short time ago she had laughed with Nell about it being her new baby.

Molly, as she drove, had the feeling she, herself, was pregnant, that the baby they had laughed about was actually hers. She smiled and imagined her soon-to-be baby girl with soft strawberry golden curls.

GOOGLE EYES

The teachers' room wasn't exactly the inspiration Sally Ann wanted for her latest writing exercise. The dirty cups, the untidy piles of books and worn out colleagues made a dismal scene.

"What are you up to?" Gillian, the English teacher had just walked in the door.

"I'm writing a story," said Sally Ann.

"I never figured you as a writer."

"Anything to forget Roger! Thought I'd give it a go. Just beginning really."

Gillian strained to look over Sally Ann's shoulder.

"I haven't written anything yet."

"Why don't you write about Roger? There's no better way to get someone out of your system."

Sally Ann closed the notebook.

"I…I'm not ready." And looking at her watch, she gasped. "Oh no, I have to run to class."

"Ha! I've got a free."

Sally didn't know how Gillian did it. She was happy in spite of students who made fun of her, in spite of the ever-increasing paperwork teachers had to do, in spite of the bad poetry sent to her by spotty adolescent boys who found her classes inspiring. It wasn't long ago that Sally Ann too was happy. The days had flown past. Teaching was challenging but also fun and then she'd be home to Roger. Rushing back to her Bedlington terrier wasn't the same.

The Tuesday night workshop didn't usually take beginners. With a room at the back of St. Mark's church, the group had been meeting for twenty years. It was quiet now as several members were away writing novels, so Sally Ann was introduced to the group by someone from her 'Roger' days, and was welcomed with open arms. The only problem was she couldn't think of what to write. 'Writers block' she supposed. In the end she managed to fill a page. The members, seated around a large antique table, took turns to read their work and have it commented on.

"Sally Ann," said the facilitator. 'Have you got anything you would like to read?"

"Well, it's not very good but…"

She read with a clear voice and when finished, looked around. Everyone was staring down at the copy she had passed around. The silence was unbearable.

A bearded gentleman at the end of the table cleared his throat.

"It's an admirable start. Thank you for sharing that with us. I'm sure your dog is very lovely."

"Yes," said a woman with frizzy brown hair. "But perhaps writing about people would be better."

'I live with my dog."

"Yes, but you could imagine."

'But I thought you were supposed to write about what you know."

"Yes…."

"Well, there was Roger."

"Roger?"

"My ex."

"Roger," they all shouted in unison. "Yes, tell us about Roger."

Sally Ann went away thinking that perhaps joining the writers' group was not such a great idea. She wanted to forget Roger not remember every detail about him. She didn't want to regurgitate their relationship for the titillation of a bunch of writers.

"What does Roger do, dear?" a rather motherly member had asked.

"He is a rock musician."

"Well, there you go, lots of material to write about. Off you go. Two pages for next week."

***

Their first meeting was in Portobello market. Sally Ann was looking at old cardigans made new by sewing silk on the cuffs and along the edges of the front. She decided to try one on, a light moss green one.

"Matches your eyes."

She thought she was hearing things. Then she heard it again and turned around. Leaning on a motorcycle was a tall apparition with long dark hair.

"Keep it on love. Then let's go get a drink."

Usually more careful, she bought the cardigan and jumped behind Roger on the motorcycle. Off they went to Henekey's! They spent the day drinking and stumbled back to her flat. He never left. When Sally Ann exposed him to her life, a cardigan life, a teacher's life, he thrived. He seemed to crave the stability.

After Roger became well known, Sally Ann was the unlikely rock girlfriend on weekends. He was constantly surrounded by hundreds of adoring females willing to perform a multitude of sexual acts on the spot. But he was an ordinary guy really, liked having his socks washed, getting a curry at the local Indian.

***

All that writing and thinking had left Sally Ann behind in some of the extra experiments she was conducting in the lab.

"What are you doing still slaving away? Go home." Gillian had changed into a sophisticated black dress and had freshened up her makeup. "Nick's picking me up to go out to dinner. I know! Why don't you come? He's bringing his colleague?"

Sally Ann looked down at work. "I can't desert my bugs. Besides I'm not dressed."

"Oh, come on. Your bugs will wait."

"All right. But you're not setting me up!"

"Wouldn't think of it! But he is single."

"What's this guy do?"

"Mel's an Engineer."

"Arr! I started going out with Roger to get rid of an engineer."

"A bit like the old lady and the fly, isn't it?"

"What? Oh yes. She swallowed the spider to catch the fly…"

At dinner Gillian told Mel that Sally Ann was writing a story, and he asked her if she would consider writing it on a blog.

"What's the story about?" he asked.

"My ex."

Sally Ann expected him to be shocked but he didn't bat an eye. On Saturday they met while he set up her blog, and told her how to upload photos and post her story about Roger!

Sally Ann's smart friends told him things he used in his songs. She had actually liked Roger's music, especially the one about her bugs called Love in the Petrie Dish. Even though he was a bit of a home-bird, as Roger gained fame, he had to tour more and more. Tied to a steady teaching job, Sally Ann wasn't able to accompany him. Anyway, she was finding the pace hard to keep up with. Roger bought her a dog, the Bedlington, to keep her company when he was away. When he played at home, she would go to see him perform. Then there was a new singer in the band. A girl. Young. Pretty. Wild. It was inevitable.

Sally Ann brought the next instalment to the writers' group before publishing it on her blog. Apart from the usual initial silence, two of the younger members whispered and giggled in the corner. The man with the beard looked stern.

"Do you want to share something with us?"

Looking down at the paper, they mumbled something inaudible.

"What's that?" asked the man.

One of them looked at Sally Ann bashfully.

"We were just wondering…you know."

"Oh just come out with it. Speak clearly."

"We were just wondering what he was like in bed."

Sally Ann jumped up from the table.

"Always the same. That's why we never had a chance. Roger oozes sexuality. Girls flock after him. It was hard for him to resist."

"He left you?"

"He didn't leave me. He'd have been happy to stay with me forever. But I'd have had to put up with the girls."

Sally Ann gave up going to the writers' group after that, and just concentrated on posting her blog. She did find the exercise therapeutic and half expected Roger to contact her, but he didn't. However, someone out of her past did surface! Because it seemed somewhat like a diary, Sally Ann forgot that it was for the public eye, and was shocked when an old ex, a long-forgotten engineer got in touch.

"How did you find me?" she emailed.

"Google."

She should have known. He was the one who had hired a private detective to find her after she had broken up with him and deliberately disappeared. At that time she'd said to the detective: "You've found me. What now?" The detective had shrugged. Now after all this time she emailed the engineer himself: "You've found me. Now what?"

"I read your blog. I thought you'd based your main character on me."

"And you are a rock star...?"

"Well, no. But I see some similarities."

"It isn't you."

"Well, it should be."

"Engineers!"

The students usually helped clean the equipment in the lab, but they were in the middle of studying for exams, so Sally Ann let them go. She liked being alone in the room.

"Gillian told me about your bugs."

Sally Ann was surprised to see Mel.

"I can be obsessed at times."

He seemed different. She hadn't noticed the gentle look in his eyes before. As if he knew what she was thinking, he said: "Contacts. I lost my glasses again."

"I know what that's like," she said.

He helped her finish cleaning the lab and then he took her to a quiet bar where he told her that he had entered her into a blog competition, and that she was one of the finalists.

"What are you doing Friday week?"

Sally Ann shrugged.

"Well, I have two tickets for the Media Awards ceremony, and I thought you'd like to go, that is if you don't mind going with me."

Something niggled at the back of Sally Ann's head.

"I don't know."

"You have a real chance of winning. People are blown away with the photos and scans of memorabilia."

"What about the writing?"

"Oh, of course, that too."

"I don't know. I've been thinking of stopping. I thought it was just for me. I've realized that anyone can read it. I guess I'm a private person."

"No problem. Just wait until after the awards. I'd love you to come. But it's your decision."

Although the old engineer kept writing her, Sally Ann got very good at ignoring his messages. "Write about me," he said. "Write about us."

She found herself looking in windows of formal dress wear and eventually tried on a long deep green chiffon dress. She rang Mel that night and said she hoped he hadn't given away the ticket.

"I'm thrilled," he said. "But I'll meet you there. I have a meeting before that."

Sally Ann took a glass of champagne off the silver tray as she looked for Mel in the crowd of tuxedoed men and exquisitely gowned women. Media cameras recorded everything – the gold coloured balloons, the luscious bouquets of flowers.

Mel came up behind her looking very smart and ushered her into their table in the ballroom.

"You wore your contacts," said Sally Ann.

"What? Oh, yes."

"I'm wearing mine tonight."

"And you look lovely."

Sally Ann hardly remembered her dinner, she was so nervous. They were on coffee when the master of ceremonies walked on to the stage. "Welcome to the Four Seasons Hotel." The categories seemed to go on and on. "And the winner for best blog is ... London Dives" Sally Ann didn't have time to feel disappointment. "Followed by Getting Over Roger."

Mel gave her a slight push and she went up to accept her prize. The other contestants at her table took turns getting their photo taken with her award. Mel leaned over and gave her a congratulatory kiss on the cheek. They locked eyes. Could she take another chance?

"It's great encouragement getting the award," he said.

"Oh yes," said Sally Ann. "And I have an idea for my next blog. Something tamer this time like Loving your Microbes. You'll have to help me because I want to use film and maybe sound.

"Utterly enthralling! But no more Roger?"

"Roger has been written out of my system," Sally Ann replied and, as if for the first time hearing the music of the band that followed the award presentations, pulled Mel up to dance.

AUNTS AND ANTS

"Don't say a word, Rosie!" warned Aunt Minnie, before the visit of an important official from the capital.

"Little girls are to be seen and not heard," she said twisting her long string of pearls. She looked cross already. Not at what I had done, but at all the things I might do when her friend arrived.

I had visited Aunt Minnie's house in the Montreal. It was big, on a street with other big houses and lots of trees. Brightly coloured clumps of flowers grew in the garden in different hues, sizes and fragrances. The house was full of antiques, but not like the dark heavy ones at Grandmother's. The wood was light, the wallpaper bright and the upholstery, flowery and crisp. My best table manners were always required.

We were, however, not at her house in the city, but at the family summer cottage on the east coast. To all who went there year after year, it was magic. Between the sea and the woods it was a place of freedom and close family ties. To others, it could appear a bit rough and primitive. That was what was making Aunt Minnie anxious and irritable.

I was placed on the settee by the window while she checked the bridge table; the new pack of cards, the score pads and the little fairy pencils. She examined the tea set, the trays of home-baked sweets and little napkins with an oriental flower design on the side table. She was primping in the mirror when a long black car drove into the yard. A man in uniform got out and walked around to open the door for the lieutenant governor. I had always called him the king of our small province because my aunts had told me he was the representative of the queen.

"The king of New Brunswick is here," I announced.

"I think I'll put you on the stairs while we play bridge," she whispered.

I wanted to catch a glance of the visitor but knew better than to argue with Aunt Minnie.

I shouldn't have been there at all. I should have been having a picnic on the beach with my mother, collecting milky glass, dried starfish and sea urchins or making bouquets of sea wheat. Mother would be out of the hospital soon. I was going into kindergarten in the autumn and didn't want to start school in Montreal with Aunt Minnie.

On the stairs I could hear everything but I couldn't be seen. I heard my Aunt Minnie and my other two aunts making a fuss over the man as they settled down to a game of bridge. Despite little snippets of conversation, the focus was on trumps and tricks. The man was Aunt Minnie's partner, and he said she played beautifully. They ended up winning. Then teacups were filled and the sweets were passed around.

I was getting bored and wished I had asked to wait outside instead of being trapped on the stairs. Time passed like length after length of cloth being rolled out in the fabric department of my grandfather's shop. I pretended I was there with the coloured spools of thread and bolts of material of different textures. In my game I sat with the two women who sewed in a little room at the back making curtains and cushions. They always let me have remnants to make doll clothes. They were both from the country and very religious. They always told me to count my blessings.

I stretched and watched an ant crawl under a crack between the staircase and the wall. It wasn't an ordinary ant. It was a flying one, one that we called a pismire, although I don't know if that is their real name. All at once, a plane from the nearby airbase broke the sound barrier in a practice run. It was over in a moment but another noise started from under the stairs. I slowly crept away as pismire after pismire crawled through the cracks and collected in a swarm. They started down the stairs and into the living room before I could say anything.

"Lord, it's like a swarm of locusts," said the official.

My aunt called for me to come to her. She was crying as she hugged me. I was surprised by the attention.

"Aren't you frightened?" she asked.

"They're just old pismires," I replied.

My other aunts were giggling.

"Yes, only pismires," the official said. "What excitement! I can always count on a little excitement from you Minnie. That's why I always like visiting you so much!"

We left the pismires in the house to deal with at a later time. Fresh tea was served outside on the porch, overlooking the scented lilac bush and beyond that the sea. This time I was included. I passed the sweets, was allowed to eat some, and could talk when I wanted to. The old man told lots of jokes. I still wanted to be with my mother but I then decided that Aunt Minnie wasn't so bad after all.

WHISTLE IN THE WIND

It was cold in the attic. Jenny was frightened climbing the dark rough staircase, not knowing what to expect when she got to the top. In her grandmother's house she had always imagined herself being chased by wolves up the stairways. The image still played at the back of her mind as she squeezed up the steep, narrow passageway and came to the top, really just a hole in the ceiling. Pulling herself up, she looked around for the light. A bare bulb hung down from the rafter.

Pink insulation fluff was laid bare and was, as she had often been warned, extremely dangerous. But there was something far worse! Hard pellets of mouse droppings were scattered on the floor. Jenny did not mind mice when they were quiet but once they started to move...

The room had a special feeling to it. Jenny went over to the windows and gazed down at the garden below. She wasn't really looking at anything. In a far-away mood, she imagined that it was her room – the bits of fluff covered over with thick floorboards matching the heavy old beams, sparse but with personality.

"Gran, the light's on now."

"Okay, I'm coming up."

Jenny could hear the old woman struggling to get up but didn't offer to help. She was still a strong woman, and there were some things she would let you help her with, and others that she wouldn't. Her granddaughter was now able to read those things quite well, and no longer had to put up with the phrase 'Do you not think I can do anything for myself?'

As Jenny waited, she looked around. It was so neat. Everything was crowded against the sloping walls. There were odd bits of furniture and many tea chests; some closed and others open. Moving closer, she bent down towards one of the open boxes and saw a pair of basketball shorts in emerald satin. Her mother had had five brothers. She used to hate those kinds of shorts but now found them vaguely attractive.

Gran did need a little help at the top of the stairs as it turned out. They were looking for an old photo album that had pictures of Jenny's grandfather. As he'd been a former mayor of the town, someone writing a history of the community wanted to include a picture of him when he was a young man. Gran had an idea where to look but she didn't want to come up alone in case anything happened.

Of course, Jenny had her own image of her grandfather. When she was a little girl she used to go on outings with him. They were usually jaunts to farms to haggle with farmers for a bag of manure for his peonies or a drive out to a fishing village to get his winter barrel of oysters. The trips were serious and meaningful in Jenny's mind – having given her an eye into the world of adult deals.

"We'll try this one," Gran said, pointing to an old wooden trunk.

A smell of old paper drifted out. There were yellowing newspapers and piles of photo albums.

Gran sat down on an old chair near the trunk as Jenny routed for the album. She pulled out a black cardboard covered book.

"What about this one?" Jenny said.

"Yes, that might be it," Gran replied.

The photos were brown. There were houses and people Jenny didn't know. On one page, there was a picture of a young girl with very long wavy brown hair. That kind of hair was not seen anymore. Jenny had always wanted hers that long, but with her fine straight hair, the longest she could wear it was just below her shoulders.

'Marguerita, The Convent, 1900' was pencilled in below the photograph.

"Gran, is that you?" Jenny asked.

She nodded. One of her sons had named his daughter Rita after her. He was upset when he found out that her full name was Marguerita; it was so much prettier. Some things get lost in the confusion of a big family.

"That's me," she said, 'when I was in the convent. Before I got married. Your grandfather should be on the next page."

"You were stunning!" Jenny said.

She turned the page and saw a little imp staring back at her. He had a wide mischievous smile, freckles, a long thin nose and ears that stuck out. He looked small.

Her grandparents were old, or seemed old, as long as she'd known them, but she could see that same humour and life in him in the photo as he'd had playing with his grandchildren. He would tell tall tales and make nonsensical comments like 'How's your old straw hat?' Even asleep, he was a source of entertainment. The grandchildren would count the hairs in his nose or time how long the shoe dangling on his foot would take to fall off.

Everyone had always said how much my Gran had adored Grandad, but looking at the pictures – one a romantic young woman and the other resembling a leprechaun – Jenny couldn't imagine the attraction. Though he'd got more attractive as he got older, he'd also got harder to live with.

"How did you meet Granddad?" Jenny dared to ask. She had never talked to her before about anything personal.

"It was that damn flute," she said.

Jenny didn't say anything, hoping she'd continue.

"I was in the choir at the convent when your grandfather noticed me. Someone told him I loved the flute and he took it up, practised hard and was in the choir with us within the year."

"He learned to play the flute for you?"

"That's what people say. I knew he liked me, but it was definitely the flute that won me."

"I don't remember him being musical," said Jenny.

"Oh, he played beautifully."

"When did he stop?"

"After we were married. I think it was just a thing he used to court me."

124

'How romantic!"

"No."

Gran looked out of the window.

"It was me. I made him stop. He used to come home from working at the shop and just play that darn flute. I had all these children. The flute was marvellous but it somehow didn't seem part of the real world anymore. It's hard to stay romantic."

"Oh, and where is his flute now?"

"I don't know. It used to be in the bottom drawer of his writing desk."

For years, her grandmother sat by the window waiting. It was good for Jenny. She'd had a troubled childhood, and Gran was always there. They never talked about problems; only shared homemade biscuits and talked about trivial things.

Gran moved into the spare bedroom when she was sixty after her husband almost burnt the bed, falling asleep with the electric blanket on, and a cigarette in his hand. She still dressed under her nightgown, a habit imbedded so strongly at the convent where she had been a border. However, when he stumbled up the stairs after a night of whisky she would be there to help. She got the water for him to put his false teeth in, and gave him his cough medicine and sleeping pills so he didn't overdo it, especially when he had drink taken. In the end he didn't know her, and accused her of trying to poison him.

Jenny had come back from Galway where she was attending University to stay with Gran the summer after he died. Gran must have been hurting, but she didn't say anything. Jenny didn't know if she was any help. She just wanted to be there.

They took the photo album down to the sitting room, and she asked Gran if she could look for the flute. Jenny found it at the bottom of the desk and decided to try to learn how to play it, something to do over the summer.

After buying some books on how to play the flute, Jenny practiced and practiced. It bothered Gran. The silence with only the sound of the Grandfather clock ticking was peaceful. Jenny broke through with her awful squeaks and whines. So, she exiled herself to the attic.

It wasn't frightening there anymore. Sweeping up the mouse droppings, she spread an old carpet by the window, placed an old table on it and surrounded it with a variety of chairs. She put a few pictures on the rough wooden walls and brought up her favourite books. There was a thermos of tea and Gran's biscuits to go with a china cup and saucer she had found in one of the boxes. She spent a lot of time on the flute.

Gran would spend her days sitting by the living-room window or baking biscuits. Jenny would come down in the afternoon to have lemonade or ice cream floats on the veranda. She would try to go into town at least once a day. They sat on the veranda together in the evenings because the light in the attic was not strong enough. Jenny would tell her the happenings of town. Never one for gossip, she was obliged to keep her ears open and chat to anyone who stopped her. Gran loved any news.

Summer was almost over and it was time to go back to college. Jenny asked if she could take the flute with her to keep practicing. Gran looked at her hard. Then she nodded her head.

"Okay, but don't waste all your time on that old thing. You have your studies.'

Jenny hugged her.

"I'll give you a concert when I come back again."

***

It was during one of those storms they have in the west of Ireland that Jenny met Mick. It had been a windy winter with frequent gales that kept the boats ashore. She had her flute with her to experiment answering the wind. Of course on this particular day, the sound was swallowed up by the storm. Trying to stand against the wind, she was almost blown over the bank onto the rocks below. Mick, who was out walking his dog before he started work at the Fire Station, grabbed her by the arm and pulled her to safety. He thought that she was an idiot to put herself in danger like that. But when he finally got to hear her play properly in the local pub where they often had music sessions, he was impressed.

After they got serious, thinking of her grandmother and grandfather, Jenny sometimes ranted: "I won't give up my flute for you."

"Come on to the pub" or "Come on to bed" was all he'd say.

They now have a little boy called Danny. Jenny has kept up her playing. Sometimes Mick is tired, and doesn't really want to listen, but he doesn't say anything. There are times Jenny doesn't feel like playing but she continues.

Gran passed away. The music keeps Jenny close to her, and to her grandad. She thinks of how they got together, and then thinks of her and Mick. Some day maybe Danny will meet someone through this same flute from that attic in a far-off country.

REUNION

The rain had almost caused the family to call off their visit to the local fair in the French countryside on their visit to the Loire Valley. Lillian, not acknowledging her rural roots, had crossed her fingers in hope that it would continue to be wet. However, she was not blessed this time. When the sun came out, the girls begged to go.

David, oblivious, went off to a bar with the Sunday papers and despite her reluctance, Lillian soon got caught up in the spirit of the festivities. Parts of the ground were muddy, the rest drying up under the heat. Local people greeted each other outside a stand that served food and drink. There were water-sport competitions on the lake and running contests for small children on the banks. A little boy wearing only a nappy put on a show on an empty stage. Other games included hoop throwing, darts and one that Lillian remembered well from her childhood: yellow rubber ducks floating in water, each one with a number under it. All you had to do was pick up a duck and see what prize corresponded to the number at the bottom. Everyone won something. She wanted her daughters to play but they were too old, or they thought they were.

"Ah, Mom!"

They looked at Lillian as they always did when they thought she was being childish or treating them like babies, and they left to go off and scream their heads off on the Waltzer, Tilt-a-Wheel or small roller coaster. Lillian stayed behind, not able for rides anymore. The last time she went on the big wheel, they'd stopped it to let her off. It had been on her first date with Paul just after moving to Dublin. She'd had a new job and a new boyfriend. Things were looking rosy. Except that there she was with Paul on the big wheel and with each climb and descent, she got paler and paler. The operators usually didn't stop the wheel, even for those who turned green and vomited all over the place. But they'd stopped for Lillian!

Paul had been good about it. He'd put his arm around her, and brought her to a place where she could sit down. He told her jokes, and she ended up laughing so hard that colour came back to her cheeks.

"We'll have to do this again soon," she'd said, and then burst into laughter once more.

For something to do while waiting for the girls, Lillian idly handed over a euro coin for three goes on the ducks. She picked one up and was given a comb set.

'So wonder my children think I'm immature!' she thought. 'Maybe I'm going into my second childhood.' She picked up a second duck. It had the number 5 on the bottom.

"The grand prize, a goldfish," the man behind the counter said in French as he handed her a clear plastic bag with a tiny fish swimming around. She held the bag up and watched the fish scales catch the sun.

Then suddenly she felt her stomach clench and her legs go wobbly. A woman over by the trees looked a lot like Claudia. When she first went to Dublin over twenty years ago, Lillian used to share a flat with her and Aisling. Claudia – if it was her – hadn't changed a lot. She still had a great figure, pouty mouth, large brown eyes and sleek hair.

When the woman looked in her direction, Lillian automatically put her head down and peeked through the clear plastic of the makeshift fishbowl. There was a man with her. Lillian expected it to be Paul, her Paul, the Paul Claudia had stolen from her all those years ago and caused her to leave the flat. Taking a deep breath, she wondered why it still hurt after all the years.

Oh God! It wasn't Paul at all. It was Barry with Claudia. And how he'd changed! Glasses. Checked shorts and knee socks. What ever happened to those tight jeans? 'Barry the Bullfighter' they used to call him.

The woman started to approach. It was definitely Claudia. She had the same squint men found so attractive.

"Excuse me, you look like an old friend of mine. I was wondering if ... Are you Lillian?"

"I thought it was you."

"I wasn't sure. I mean you are a lot heavier!"

"It happened after I gave up smoking."

"We're here visiting my parents. They bought an old farmhouse in the area," she said.

"I'm here on holiday with the family."

"Are you still in Dublin?"

"Yes, and you?"

"Still there."

Claudia glanced at the goldfish and the comb set and looked around for Lillian's children. She gave a smug smile and pointed to Barry and a young girl and boy.

"Those are my two," she said.

"Oh, and is that Barry? He has changed a lot. I would hardly know him."

She beamed.

"He's become, oh you know, very serious and responsible now that he has a family." Claudia was like a dog showing off its bone.

"And you, are you working?" I asked.

"I'm giving grinds. Flexible hours. You know."

Lillian was not really interested in her life so she decided to come right out with it. "Do you ever see Paul?"

"No, we really had nothing in common."

"I thought you called it destiny at the time."

Claudia looked over at her family "I'm sure Barry would love to see you again. I'll call him over."

Long-ago feelings for Paul, and Claudia's betrayal swarmed over Lillian. Suddenly she wanted to be as far away as possible from her old friend. Making her excuses, she walked away.

In a bad mood, Lillian won prize after prize playing darts. Then she remembered the time that she had given Claudia a jar of expensive beauty cream that made her face break out in spots.

"Mean," thought Lillian. "Mean but funny!"

Claudia had taken Paul but with a price. Her face had

swollen up in huge red blotches.

'She was a bit thick about some things,' Lillian thought. Perhaps Claudia felt differently, but Paul should have been off limits among roommates.

Claudia had never suspected that Lillian had tried out the face cream first and that she too had broken out. She'd thanked her profusely for the gift. Then later she was confused.

"What could be doing this to my face?" she'd asked.

"Destiny," Lillian had replied.

Claudia had looked bewildered but only said.

"Sometimes I don't seem to understand you."

Happy now with David, Lillian couldn't help thinking how her life would have been with Paul. But if he was fickle enough to fall under Claudia's spell, then it had definitely been for the best. And she had had her revenge with the face cream.

Lillian was laughing to herself when she met up with the girls. They thought she was still laughing about rubber ducks.

STRANDED

Joe said there was a golden clock inside the train station that kept good time. He said there was a stained glass dome that made you feel as if you were in a world of colours and light, like looking up to heaven. I could see heaven in my mind, but it didn't look like that. It was swirls of gold and white.

Back to the train station. Joe said inside the front door there was a reception room. You bought your tickets to one side. I already had my ticket. If I walked right through, I would be in the waiting area with shops and cafes and seats. It was easy enough.

"Come on, boy. Let's go."

Inside the station, my shoes made a clicking sound on the stone floor. I had always walked heavily. People rushed past me. The intercom told me to mind my baggage. There were thieves and pickpockets around. But I didn't have any baggage. Joe had brought everything down last Saturday. But pickpockets! A few people had bumped into me. They had said they were sorry but you never know.

"You can't bring that dog in here. Oh, sorry I didn't see your cane,' someone shouted over the noise of the engines. I stood there and waited.

"Let me see your ticket. Ah yes, track four. Is there no one to mind you?"

"My dog," I said.

"I'll get someone to help you then. Do you have to bring that beast on the train with you?"

I smiled, preferring to take the remark in a humorous vein. I told him that Kaw went everywhere with me, and was very well behaved. I could hear the static of a machine as he spoke and not long after that a woman appeared on my left side.

"Let me help you," she said.

"I'm meeting someone. They're getting on at the first stop." I said. "I just need help to get on the train."

I wanted to tell her more. I wanted to describe our wedding in the church with windows of the saintliest blue and reds redder than blood, with chandeliers and a hundred candles, and the fragrance of flowers as I walked up the aisle to my Joe, how he described it to me.

I know he is handsome because I have touched his face. He fills in the colours. His straight dark hair bounces intently over deep brown eyes. I think he must have a romantic look, Victorian, but not the stuffed-shirt type. Definitely not the stuffed shirt type! I looked forward to the honeymoon.

"Thanks for catching me," I said to the woman beside me.

"It was an umbrella someone left behind. Careless," she said.

The women's name was Jenny; not that she told me, but I heard someone calling to her. She passed me over to the conductor who helped me onto the train, and helped Kaw too. He guided us to an empty compartment. The whistle blew. I was seated by the window. I could feel the coolness of glass near my cheek.

Others opened the door and asked if they could join me. I nodded. One of them asked if my dog was cross. I just patted Kaw's head.

Joe had said that the train would be leaving at six o'clock on the dot. He said it would take an hour to get to stop where he would meet me on the train, and that we would continue on to our new home to begin life together by the sea.

My new husband had helped me to sell my house and all my furniture. He bought this lovely little cottage for us. He said it had windows with a view of the sea on each side. Around the house were flowers of blue and other colours I recognised from when I could still see. He said I would be able to manage to get around in the house in no time.

There seemed to be a delay in setting off. There are times that I just have to cry out in the wilderness, just say something, and wait for someone, anyone to answer.

"What time is it?" I asked. A man with a calm voice answered, "Sorry, I don't have a watch."

"What about that big golden clock in the station?" I said. "Can you see it from here?"

"What big clock in the station?"

'The big one made of gold."

I said it in a way that implied that he was stupid. I took a deep breath.

"There's a clock in the station that is made of pure gold

136

and keeps perfect time and rings out a little melody every quarter hour."

Come to think of it, I had not heard any melody but that could be because there were so many other new sounds to distract me.

"I take this train once a week. I know the station well. There is no golden clock," said the man. "This is a modern station. All the clocks are digital."

I didn't know what to say.

"I'll go and find out the time for you."

The man could see I was upset. I reached out for him and caught his arm

"Just a minute," I said weakly. "Does this station have a glass dome?"

I already knew what the answer would be. Joe had been my eyes for the last six months. It had been like putting on rose-coloured glasses. He painted everything beautiful for me, doubtless just as beautiful as his canvasses. But those images were not mine, and sadly I realized they were not real. Kaw and I were on our own.

HE GAVE THE DOG A KICK

There are certain phrases or actions that tell us that a person has passed the limit of being acceptable, and it is better to keep one's distance. In Hollywood, this was once portrayed by kicking a dog and has been replaced, in recent years, by the lighting of a cigarette or a particular accent. These supposedly demonstrate that the character is beyond salvation.

I've always wanted to believe in the intrinsic good of everyone. I see warning signs but always wait to the end, to just before I am in danger of becoming that dog about to be kicked.

This time I knew from the beginning to be careful. He phoned to make a reservation at the small hotel in the west of Ireland where I was working. We talked for a long time. (He worked for the French Telephone Company). We had all the arrangements made, and I quoted him the final price. He argued that that it was much cheaper in the brochure he held in front of him. Although I tried to explain that the brochure was several years old, he was adamant and I finally gave in. It was off-season anyway and the hotel could do with the business. I arranged to have Monsieur Malherbe picked up at the airport, and didn't see him until the next day. He was a small man with white hair, no neck and a permanent sheepish grin. He was a man it was difficult to be nice to.

The hotel had a family atmosphere and the guests readily mixed with one another, exploring the wild landscape and pub life. I noticed that both the guests and the hotel staff were distancing themselves from the little Frenchman.

He spoke passable English. I would ask him what he'd been doing. "Nothing" was always his response, and with a pout and various gesticulations and noises, he would go on to complain about the weather. Admittedly, it was dreadful but the other guests were so active and sociable, they didn't seem to mind.

After his first week, he started speaking French to me. I suppose this was a reaction to the expression on my face whenever he spoke. Whenever we had a chat, I could actually feel a blank stare form itself on my face, and my mouth drop. No sound would come out. It was not the language. It was the outrageous things he said.

Meals were provided with the room, as we were rather isolated. One morning, Monsieur arrived down to the lobby later than usual. The restaurant was being set up for lunch. Not changing his smiling expression, he declared that he had missed his breakfast. I offered to serve him toast and coffee in the sunroom.

He started rubbing his fingers in a strange way and asked, "Can I have money?"

I was speechless. Every morning he repeated the same

request. I'm afraid speaking in French didn't help much as my expression remained the same.

It was the last weekend before he was due to leave. He was going to Dublin for a visit. I had provided him with information on fares and times of buses. As it was my day off that Saturday, I was driving to meet some friends at a pub when I passed Monsieur standing on the side of the road holding a sign saying Dublin. He was still there several hours later when I was on my way home.

Monsieur Malherbe took small steps down a dark empty alley. He saw the butt of a cigarette on the ground, picked it up and lit it. A small Cairn terrier – my dog – was sniffing through rubbish, intent on some imaginary hunt. Monsieur's tiny pointed shoe caught him in the side and threw him up.

I woke up shaking and decided to catch 10 o'clock mass. Outside the church excited little girls in white darted with their frilly communion dresses and veils. Near the back I noticed Monsieur with his sinister little smile. I nodded and went my own way. He couldn't have gone to Dublin after all.

The next morning he appeared brimming with excitement. He had something in his hand that he wanted me to see. But he just couldn't bring himself to release his grasp on it. Finally, he held it up so that the sun made it shine. He polished it on his sleeve. It was a bright new gold Communion medal with an inscription on the back. I imagined the tears that must have flowed from small eyes after the loss of such a treasure.

He started to speak. "I want...."

I interrupted him saying it was kind of him, that some

girl or boy would be so happy it had been found. I suggested we tell the Gardai and put up a notice in the church and schools. I offered to try to find its owner.

"It shouldn't be so hard. Not with the inscription," I said.

'No," he said. 'You don't understand. I sell. Money. I want only the money!"

A FINE THREAD

The comic was still inside the Maine Tourist guide under her pillow. The big bed had clean smelling sheets and a flowery bedspread. She turned off the television and crawled under the covers. Extracting the Maine guide from under the pillow, she took the comic out but kept the magazine close in case she had to put it away again quickly.

Thumbing through the pages to decide which story she would read first, she settled on one called, *The Gentleman of the Closet.* With a glance at the wardrobe in the room, she checked that its door was closed before she began reading.

There was an old house Ted visited delivering groceries. Whenever he arrived, a voice would tell him to go in, put down the box, pick up an envelope for the shop and take his tip. There was always a man in the hall closet. He wore a long beige trench coat and had on a wide-brim brown felt hat pulled down low, covering his face.

"I can never seem to find my damn walking stick," was the reason he gave for being in the closet.

Nothing had happened, and yet Bonnie's heart was racing. She sat up and closed the comic book. She knew she should stop there. She actually got up, turned off the light and tried to sleep. But she found herself lying there wondering how the story finished.

She couldn't stand it anymore. She had to see what happened. Jumping up, she turned on the light and whipped the comic from under her pillow. Outside, trees cast shadows on the window and a light wind mixed with irregular night sounds of revelry.

The boy had become a regular at the big house.

"You always catch me when I am going out. And I can never find that blasted walking stick."

After Ted got accustomed to the man, he no longer felt apprehension on entering the house. He did, however, desperately hope that the man's hat would move back a little so that he could see his face. One day, he left the box on the entrance table and collected the envelope and his tip. The man was in the closet as usual looking for his walking stick.

"There it is," the man said. "If only I could bend down just a little further. The old back's not what it used to be."

"I'll help you," Ted piped up.

"That would be nice," said the old man.

He moved aside to let the boy squeeze in. Ted spotted the walking stick on the floor towards the back. He picked it up and turned to see if he could get a look at the old gentlemen's face. A reflection made the man's eyes shine red from under his hat. Ted picked up the stick and his movement caused the man to shuffle a bit. Ted was in luck. The hat slipped from the man's head. A scream caught in Ted's throat as sticky thread artfully wrapped around his body.

"Thanks," said the man. Ted saw the giant hairy legs just before the fibre covered his eyes, and left him tied up in the dark.

Bonnie couldn't think of anything else except the monster. She looked over to the closet, which seemed to radiate pure evil. With the light still on, she got up and put a chair in front of its door. She pulled the blanket high up under her chin and laid there, eyes wide, watching and waiting. She hid the comic under her cotton pyjama top and recalled how anxious she had been to get rid of her parents. Now she wished that they would walk in the door.

She must have drifted off because it was suddenly dark. Someone had turned off the lights. Her parents were talking quietly in the bed next to hers.

"I think we should tell her as soon as possible," her mother whispered.

"There's time enough to tell her," her father argued softly.

"But she has a right to know."

"We don't want to ruin the holiday," her father insisted.

Her mother started to raise her voice. "But I've never hidden anything from her."

"Sh! Marjorie, it's our last one together. Let her enjoy it."

Her mother let out a long sigh. "Perhaps you're right. The holiday will soften the blow.'

Worried that the fighting would start again, Bonnie had been concentrating more on their tone than on what they were saying. Now sensing a calmness, she turned over on her side ready to fall back to sleep. But out of the corner of her eye, she saw the door of the closet swing open, exposing the darkness inside.

Her screams brought people from other rooms to see what was wrong. While her father talked to them convincing them she was fine, her mother jumped up and hugged her.

"Was it your nightmare?' she asked.

Bonnie clung to her and nodded slowly.

Her mother looked at her closely.

"You didn't buy that comic, did you?" she asked.

She'd felt the rolled-up bulk of paper under the thin material of her pyjama top.

"Oh, Bonnie, you know you shouldn't have. What got into your head?"

Bonnie expected to be told off, but her mother just held her tighter.

"You're alright. You're alright." she kept repeating like a lullaby, tears falling down her face.

In the morning her father made her tear up the comic. For the following two weeks her dreams consisted of whales breaking the surface of the water and then plummeting back into the deep. The wonder of seeing the large mammals was just as strong in her sleep as it had been when she stood at the side of the boat with foamy spray hitting her face. Little oriental girls also entered her nights after she had seen *The Flower Song* in an outdoor theatre and another dream was formed from the patchwork quilts, wood carvings and corn husk dolls she had seen in the many craft shops.

They were home in Nova Scotia about a week when her father called her in from the little wood in the back of their house where she had been playing. Her mother was sitting up straight on the sofa. Her father put her on his knee.

"Bonnie, there's something we have to tell you,' he said stroking her forehead. 'But before that I want to make sure

145

that you know that we both love you very much. And you mustn't think it is anyway your fault."

She pulled away.

"Nooooo," she shouted running to her room and locking the door behind her. She lay on the bed, hands over her ears and turned over on her side. The closet door was open. Her party dresses were hanging there, and on the floor, pairs of old shoes were lined up. She got up to close the door. Her hand was on the doorknob but she thought she heard something at the back. When she went in to check it out, the door closed quietly after her.

"Thank you," she heard someone say in a cultured masculine voice. Then the silky thread covered her ears, and there she was – all tucked in and cosy.

THE MEETING

Ellen Harper looked up at the gold-coloured office block. The sun was shining on the glass making the whole area feel warm and rich. On one side a river flowed quickly out to the sea providing rides for the ducks and swans.

"I wish I could just sit on a swan's back and go riding down that river," she thought.

It was early for the meeting. Waiting, the golden glass caught her reflection. She looked good. Red clothes are not supposed to go with red hair, but her suit was cut well, and what the hell anyway. Red was her favourite colour and made her feel good. The hair could be a bit longer though; she looked too much like an elf with it that short. Not exactly the business image she wanted to project.

Why did they have to send her? She was hopeless. Last time it ended up costing the company. Not much, mind you. But still. They were always insisting that everybody be involved in sales, whether good at it or not. There were so many other things she was better at.

It was time to go in. Fingers crossed that the sun would still be shining when she came out. Maybe she'd have lunch down by the river.

"Where is Suite 236?' she asked a heavy set man with bushy eyebrows seated behind the reception desk.

"There is no office with that number," he answered.

"What do you mean? I have a meeting there this morning," Ellen looked at her watch. "Right now to be exact."

The security man shook his head.

"Not that office. It hasn't been built yet. What company are you here to visit?"

Ellen frowned. "O-de-Dog Perfume!"

"They are in Suite 136."

"That's odd," said Ellen, "I could have sworn they said 236."

"They have been in 136 for five years now. Room 236 may be built by next week but it's not available for use at the moment. I'll show you the way to the right room."

Ellen followed the guard down to the coffee machine, then left, along a corridor and down some stairs. It was the third door on the right. He showed her into the room and left, closing the door. She waited on a chair in the empty room and thought about her presentation.

O-de-Dog was an upmarket company that manufactured safe and pleasing scents to mask the unsavoury odour of pets. After five years of selling to an exclusive clientele, it was ready to launch itself on the world, and it was her job to land the promotion contract.

Ellen's boss thought she was the right person to send because she liked dogs, but as a dog-lover, Ellen would never use the perfume. She loved the comforting animal smell of her Labrador. Except when he was wet (or had run into a skunk). No, this product was better aimed at the kind of person who bought themselves expensive perfume, cosmetics and clothes and thought it perfectly normal that they should do so for their pets. The promotion would not be aimed at the dogs but at their owners.

"Spoiled," Ellen thought.

She shook her head. Better not think like that if she wanted to win the contract.

Her real job at the agency was copy editing, until her boss came up with the new policy of everyone participating in sales.

She could picture a dog getting out of a limousine with its owner, a beautiful woman, to the pulsing rhythm of trendy music. It would have to be the right kind of dog. An afghan would look good, but is too stupid. Nor would she like something too cute and cuddly. A Dalmatian maybe, with a jewelled collar. A crowd would rush over to the woman. An attractive man would sniff the air and say, "Oh la la, it's O de Dog". The woman would wrap her arm around the dog, stand up, take the man's arm. and they would walk together into the music awards.

Ellen looked at her watch. Nothing was happening in this room, so she decided to go and see if she could find someone in the company. She ended up going up one floor to look for room 236. And there it was! She slipped in, closing the door quietly behind her. She wondered why the security guard had tried to mislead her.

The room could have been anywhere. There was a round table that could seat six, with a pitcher of water and glasses in the middle. Pads of paper and pens were set out at each place. Everything else was nondescript. Bland copies of flower prints hung indifferently on oatmeal-coloured walls. There were no logos, no letterhead nor any sign that showed that this was the company she was looking for.

Ellen helped herself to a glass of water, sat down and looked out at the river. The outside wall was all glass. The river was very high. There had been a lot of rain over that week. Before today that is! Today was sunny.

Twenty minutes late for the meeting and still no one came. She was beginning to think that, although the security guard seemed crazy, he was right.

"I'll go ask someone else," she thought.

The doorknob wouldn't turn. She jiggled it back and forth then banged on the door.

"Hello, I'm locked in this room," she shouted.

Tired and helpless, she turned to the window. The sun had gone. Dark clouds were swelling, and finally burst into heavy rain. The river continued to rise, and flowed faster than ever until it overflowed. Water poured onto the cement concourse. Ellen stared at it, mesmerized.

She tried the door again. Would she ever get out of there? Where was everybody else? With a chair propped by the door, she waited to see if she could hear if anyone passed.

The water kept rising up from the overflowing river and heavy rain. Ellen watched it climb up the outside glass wall until she was beginning to feel like a goldfish. It was happening too quickly. Where was everyone?

"I have a great slogan for O-de Dog Perfume," she shouted in the empty room. "Dogs with confidence. Dogs with O-de-Dog."

The water now reached about a quarter of the way up the glass wall of the room.

There was a strange sound from the outside. Whooz, whooz, Swans' wings beat in unison. Whooz. Whooz. Then the swans got into formation, arched up and attacked the glass. A small crack appeared in the bottom.

Terrified, Ellen tried the door again. She tried a variety of ways: turning it quickly and forcefully back and forth, sneaking up on it and turning it in one quick jerk and pushing and turning at the same time. The door opened finally after many attempts.

Ellen ran downstairs. The same security guard was sitting behind the reception desk reading a newspaper. Sun was pouring in through the glass doors.

"Thank God the rain has stopped," said Ellen. "If that window in 236 had been exposed to any more attacks by swans or the elements, it would have been a disaster."

The guard looked up to heaven.

"How many times do I have to tell you? 236 does not exist."

END OF THE LINE

The puck shot into the net with just seconds to go, gaining a win for the college team, which would now go on to play the Russians at the Forum in Montreal. It was the first time that a college team would compete in ice hockey against the Russians. Kelly still felt the excitement as she went back to the university residence and put on some music. Her buxom roommate, Donna, came in from working at Gentleman Wynne's, a local bar and restaurant.

"You missed a great game," Kelly said, jumping up and down. "We're going to Montreal!"

"Who got the goal?" asked Donna.

"Who do you think?" answered Kelly, and they both swooned.

Later, lying in bed with the lights out, Kelly found it hard to fall asleep. She looked forward to going to Montreal with her friends for the game the following week. However, she couldn't make up her mind on another matter.

Kelly's father lived in Montreal. She had been corresponding with him ever since she moved to Kingston, Ontario, to attend university. She was curious, not having seen him since her parents broke up when she was seven.

The reason for the separation, she thought, was something to do with her but she wasn't sure what it was. Should she call him and arrange a meeting? She just didn't know.

Kelly closed her eyes and tried to remember him but only came up with two things – the fact he liked liquorice, and that he was very tall with a handsome face. Her mother had burnt all the photographs of him so she had to rely totally on memory. Still it was important to know where one came from. If it didn't work out, at least her university friends, in Montreal for the hockey game, would be there to support her.

The Montreal Forum ice rink was packed. Kelly was dressed in her black velvet mini-skirt and pink angora sweater with matching earmuffs. She wanted to look good when she met her father at the restaurant afterwards. The clothes were not enough to keep her warm, sitting there on the bleachers so she was delighted to join the crowd every time they got up and cheered, gaining warmth from the movement and close bodies. The game was much tamer than she had hoped because the Russians played 'clean'. Her team played 'dirty' as usual and won.

They were to meet in the bar of a pseudo-British pub on Crescent St. in the centre of town.

"I'm here to meet Richard Vanier," Kelly told a man dressed as an English butler. However, she didn't wait for a response. Strangely enough, she recognised her father right away sitting in the corner smoking a cigarette. She could see the familiar robin-egg blue cigarette packet lying on the table. Things were coming back to her.

He was a little more portly than she remembered, but was still tall and straight as an arrow. His handsome face greeted her with light, clear blue eyes that were a reflection of her own. His hair still sported the little monk's bald spot that was a source of amusement to her as a child. He stood up when she reached him, always the perfect gentleman.

After a drink, they took a taxi to Old Montreal. The restaurant was one of those French bistros with thick stone walls and quaint décor typical to Quebec. The area was cobble-stoned with narrow windy streets lined with art galleries and restaurants. Surprisingly, she met someone she knew from her hometown in the Maritimes working there as a waiter. There were never any secrets from that place!

Expensive restaurants had a strong attraction for her that year. She was convinced that she would meet the perfect young executive, or the right contact for the perfect job at one of them. Her first year away from home also made her try to be more sophisticated as she was certain that would help bring bright future after she finished university.

Dinner was spent answering a lot of questions. After all, it had been 11 years. Little was said about her mother and she was pleased, feeling this meeting was a slight betrayal, disloyalty to the woman, and maybe even to herself. She was not quite sure.

Her father had been doing research on her ancestors and spent much of the time talking about them, even showing her pictures. The sepia images showed men standing erect in ancient military uniforms and women posing in long Persian lamb coats with curls piled high on their heads.

Kelly was polite, but felt no connection with the pillars of society of whom he seemed so proud. Later, she realised that because she was the end of her family line, she was the one who was supposed to remember. It was not a role she wanted to play.

They were on their coffee when he reached over to an empty seat and picked up a gift-wrapped package. The present inside, was exquisite, but not at all what she had expected, and perhaps not really appropriate for someone just gone eighteen. Although she made the appropriate noises while holding up the red lace negligee, she quickly put it away, feeling embarrassed.

Back in Kingston, she was secretive about the meeting when her friends asked about it in the days that followed. She tried on the negligee when she was sure no one would burst in her room, but she felt uncomfortable and took it off quickly. Her roommate Donna would have died for something like it. Kelly would gladly have given it to her, but then she would have to explain how she got it.

Better to dispose of it! She tied the nightgown up in a plastic bag, walked into the night and tossed the bundle in the used clothes bin. If she had to be the end of the line, it wouldn't be wearing lace.

SUNBEAM

Brendan always had a smile for me when we met. So when I saw him across the street on that afternoon of rain, I felt cheerful. He crossed over when he saw me, his smile in place.

"I was just going to have a coffee," he said.

I had planned to go home but said I'd join him as soon as I brought my books back to the library and tied the dog to an ornamental tree in front of the café. He put away the newspaper he was reading when I walked in. The waiter brought two black coffees and a croissant with chocolate sauce dripped onto it.

"I'm waiting for the bus," he said, still smiling. "The car is in for servicing."

I always thought of Brendan as somewhat boyish. It could have been that smile. Or perhaps it was his pale skin, his slight form or his clear blue eyes. Yet none of that would count if it weren't for his youthful enthusiasm. We meet by accident from time to time although I don't know him well. He kept me up to date with his life: his work with the art gallery, a year in New York, the Masters at Queens, the move to the Gaeltacht.

***

One summer during the Arts Festival, I was standing outside of Moon's Department Store, now Brown Thomas, watching a group of blue men from Australia. They were sitting in the shop window without moving. Rumour had it that one was a fake, a mannequin, and everyone was staring at them to try to spot which one. I turned around in the crowd and there was Brendan, smiling. When I approached him, I noticed a slender girl with long brown hair at his side.

"You know Nollaig?" he asked, as a form of introduction.

I turned to offer her my hand. Nollaig flashed the most beautiful smile and looked into my eyes with warmth and interest. She and Brendan were definitely a pair!

***

I watched him bite into the croissant with envy. I was on a diet.

"Any closer to buying a house?" I asked.

He shrugged. "Can't get a mortgage. We're self-employed. Banks don't want to know us."

He managed a weak smile. Then he perked up.

"I have an exhibition next month." It was his first solo project.

"You know Pierce and Cliodhna had a baby," he said.

"Yes, I saw him. Beautiful baby. Very good too."

Brendan looked shy. Head down, in a whisper he said: "We're going to have one too. In August."

They almost seemed too young to be parents. Then a picture came into my head of a baby between them, its mouth in a warm happy smile. I couldn't help but feel good about the world.

"Congratulations," I said.

As I got up to go, a sunbeam streaked through the large café front window catching Brendan on the chest where his heart was.

- fin -

Gaelóg Press